The Silver Sea

Debby Fowler

Best wishes

[signature]

A Felicity Paradise crime novel

ISBN 978 185022 223 1

Published by Truran, Croft Prince, Mount Hawke,
Truro, Cornwall TR4 8EE
www.truranbooks.co.uk

Truran is an imprint of Truran Books Ltd

Thanks: the usual group of victims need to step
forward and be counted – Jo, who types my
manuscripts, Sally who acts as courier, Heather and
Ivan wonderfully long suffering and patient editors,
my family and the Stevens – Caroline, Nigel and
Tony, who photographed the book cover before his
death just over a year ago. Thank you so much for
your support.

Printed and bound in Cornwall by R. Booth Ltd,
The Praze, Penryn, TR10 8AA

www.felicityparadise.com

This book is dedicated to the orphanage children of Romania.

PROLOGUE

March 2005, St Ives, Cornwall

Archie was not a thing of beauty. He was, however, much loved. His mistress, not quite so besotted as his master, privately referred to him as a 'labradoodle' which was quite a good description as Archie appeared to be an exotic mix of poodle and Labrador – his stance and shape being that of a Labrador, while his coat was a riot of brindle curls and his tail ... well, the less said about his tail, the better. However, it was Archie's expression, which enslaved people, his kind brown eyes did indeed appear to be the windows to his soul. He had the habit of smiling cheerfully upon introduction, and affected a predominately quizzical look, which suggested that he found the antics of his human companions both comical and endearing.

So it was that one afternoon in late March, Archie and his master, Henry Sinclair, were idling their way along Porthmeor Beach. The tide was in and after a blustery couple of weeks, both man and dog were enjoying the tranquillity of a calm sea and a gentle breeze. Henry was deep in thought, planning the planting programme for his tiny greenhouse, and so he was some way along the beach before he noticed that Archie was no longer with him. He stopped and whistled; Archie did not come. Over the mound of sand, which had been created by the high tide at equinox, he heard Archie bark. It was definitely a command – 'Come here, I have something to show you'. With a sigh Henry turned, retraced his steps, and climbed up over the mound of sand below Porthmeor Studios to find Archie standing guard over a pile of discarded beachwear which, on close inspection, proved to be a board bag, a towel and a pair of flip-flops. Archie barked again and anxiously scanned Henry's face for understanding.

Henry looked at the board bag and at Archie and shook his head. 'What's all this about, old boy? Nothing unusual here,' he said soothingly.

Archie wasn't having it, he barked again. Henry slowly turned from the dog and looked out to sea; his eyes scanned the full length of the beach. There was no one in the water; the tide was too far in for surfing. He stepped away from the wall of the studios and looked upwards towards the deserted beach café, there was certainly no sign of life. Once again he turned and scanned the water, looked up and down the beach and then returned his gaze to Archie, who gave him an encouraging bark as if to say, 'Heaven's above, you took your time catching on.'

'So you're worried about this surfer, Archie?' Henry asked.

Archie wagged his tail enthusiastically. 'Come on then, we'll go up onto the Island and have another look at the beach from there and if we still can't spy him, we'll tell the coastguards.'

Satisfied that some action was being taken and with a last sniff at the towel, Archie abandoned his post and trotted off ahead along the beach with Henry in pursuit.

From their vantage-point on the Island, Henry and Archie stood and stared along the full length of Porthmeor Beach. There was no sign of life, literally; nobody was about. Even the beach road below the Tate was deserted. Henry's gaze swept the sea again, squinting against the light. There was nothing to see but a couple of cormorants apparently involved in a diving competition. With the sea as calm as it was, it would have been easy to pick out a surfer.

'Looks like you're right, old boy. Come on then, let's report your concern,' said Henry.

They were just packing up for the day at the lookout post on the other side of the Island.

'Archie here reckons you've got a missing surfer,' said Henry.

'Oh, he does, does he?' said the coastguard, looking none too impressed.

'He's not normally wrong about this sort of

thing,' added Henry, having explained Archie's find on the beach.

'Well, I'll certainly make a note of it,' said the coastguard, 'but I'm sure you'll appreciate that discarded beachwear is not exactly an unusual feature on Porthmeor.'

'No, of course not,' said Henry, 'but it is surely slightly more unusual at this time of year when the tide is in and there is no one in the water.'

'He probably went home after his surf and forgot he'd left his stuff behind. He'll be back for it later, when he remembers.'

'Archie doesn't think so,' Henry persisted.

'Like I say,' said the coastguard, 'I will make a note of Archie's view,' his voice heavy with sarcasm.

Just after five o'clock on the same evening, the coastguards received a call from the local police. Lady Irving, wife of Sir Hugo, was worried about her husband who had gone surfing on Porthmeor and had not returned home. 'Probably in the pub,' the policeman grumbled, 'but we've made some preliminary enquiries around town and certainly can't spot him. Culdrose will need to put up a helicopter right away, it'll be dark soon.'

Half an hour later the lifeboat was launched. Felicity Paradise, sitting at her kitchen table sketching, paused briefly as she heard the rocket go up. She glanced across at Orlando, her enormous and ancient marmalade cat, who was sitting on a chair by the Aga.

'Some poor soul is in trouble, Orlando,' she said. 'Aren't we lucky to be tucked up in the warm?'

Orlando regarded her with his usual scary stare and resumed licking his paws.

At dawn the following morning a fisherman on his way out of St Ives Bay spotted a broken surfboard which was soon identified as belonging to Sir Hugo Irving, since it had been custom-built for him. By lunchtime the national press had descended on St Ives, shaking the little town out of its late winter inertia, as camera crews set up along the beach, interviewed local surfers and fishermen about the likely fate of Sir Hugo and plagued the life out of the harbourmaster. The Sloop Inn was suddenly busy again, the restaurants had custom at last after the commercial desert which had been January and February. There was almost a festive air in the town.

Sir Hugo Irving, banker, financier and now hugely successful industrialist, knighted the previous year for his services to British industry, was a high profile flamboyant figure. He was one of those people who could enter a crowded room and instantly dominate it. He was loud, brash and ruthless in business but he also had a softer side, a philanthropic nature. The press were surprised by the number of people who came forward expressing real sorrow at his apparent demise, for during the next three days no body was found. After the initial flurry of activity by the rescue services, there was a nine-day wait. A body which sinks on drowning is either swept out to sea or supposedly takes nine days to come back up to the surface, a bloated, gruesome spectacle. Tension to the point of excitement built as the ninth day approached, but no body bobbed to the surface.

Gradually the press drifted away, the widow-in-waiting returned to the Irvings' London home and the town began gearing itself up for Easter. Archie seemed to have taken his brief moment of famein his stride and was happy to return to his main passion in life which was fruitlessly and pointlessly chasing seagulls across the beach, splashing happily through rock pools with inappropriate enthusiasm. Of Sir Hugo Irving there remained no sign, no trace, no body, no explanation.

1

July 2005, The Isles of Scilly

Felicity Paradise, normally an unrepentant sun worshipper, moved under the shade of an umbrella. It was extremely hot and still, unusual for Scilly where there was normally some breeze. She was sitting in the Abbey Garden café on Tresco trying to relax over a coffee. It was not easy. Her grandsons were running between the tables, backwards and forwards, chasing the sparrows, which were always close at hand on Tresco. They were having a great time but not, Felicity suspected, proving particularly popular with fellow customers.

Felicity was in charge of the boys today. They were a delightful but noisy hyperactive pair, and she had sensed that Jamie, her son, and Trish his wife could do with a day together, away from the demands of their children. Besides, she loved the boys and didn't see nearly enough of them so it was no hardship to spend the day with them.

She leaned forward for a better view of them. They were standing in a patch of sunlight crumbling up a scone and feeding tiny pieces to a group of appreciative sparrows who had gathered on an empty table. Sam, seven now, was tall and rangy like his Australian mother, a good-looking boy and from his already angular features it was possible to see the man he would become ... and then there was Harry, five last week. Harry was the very image of Charlie, Felicity's husband who had been dead now for three years. He had the same roly-poly face and stature and the same shock of white blonde hair. He also had Charlie's sense of humour and the same love of life. Under her scrutiny Harry looked up and smiled at her – he even had Charlie's easy charm, too. Felicity's heart lurched, quick tears came into her eyes and she hurriedly blinked them away.

It was a long time since she had cried for Charlie and whole days went by now when she barely thought of him. However, since they had come to Tresco, he had been very much on her mind. Maybe it was the constant reminder created by Harry or maybe it was that tomorrow was her fiftieth birthday, a watershed birthday, and although she would have her family around her, she was very conscious that she was without a life partner. Here she was at fifty, alone and likely to remain so.

'Granny, come and look!' Sam was calling her.

Reluctantly Felicity rose to her feet and winced. They had spent the morning cycling around Tresco and rediscovering her cycling muscles was proving a torturous business. She hobbled over to where the boys were feeding the birds.

'Look, Granny, aren't they lovely, they're so tame,' Sam said.

'They are. They're enjoying that scone.'

'Can we go biking again now, Granny?' Harry asked, clearly he felt the sparrows had been adequately catered for.

'Yes, of course,' said Felicity, trying not to wince, 'where do you want to go now?'

'The shop,' they both chorused.

Living in the wilds of Oxfordshire, being able to bike around Tresco and do their own shopping was something of a novelty for Sam and Harry.

'We'll go to the shop and pick up some pasties and then we'll have lunch on the beach and a swim.'

'Yeh,' shouted Sam, running out of the garden and through the café towards their waiting bikes.

Harry slipped his hand into Felicity's. 'We're having a nice holiday, aren't we Granny?' he said, regarding her with Charlie's eyes.

A warm glow chased away the morbid thoughts of a moment ago. 'We certainly are, Harry,' she assured him.

July 10th was another warm and sunny day on Tresco but mercifully the breeze was back. Mel, Felicity's daughter, arrived on the first helicopter and by eleven o'clock, the family was assembled for Bucks Fizz and croissants on the terrace of their rented cottage overlooking Old Grimsby. The table was piled high with presents and cards. A great effort clearly had been made to make Felicity feel special, and she did. Before starting on her presents, she opened her cards. There was a surprising number – from old friends and work colleagues in Oxford and from her new friends in St Ives. The last card she opened was a breathtaking photograph of Porthminster beach at dawn, the blues, greens and apricots exquisite, the white sand tinged by a reddened sky. Entranced she opened the card. 'To Felicity Paradise, very best wishes on your special day. Keith Penrose, (Chief Inspector).'

'Goodness,' said Felicity, 'promotion, he'll be far too smart to talk to me now.'

'Who, Mum?' Mel enquired.

'Inspector Penrose is Inspector Penrose no longer, he is now Chief Inspector Penrose.'

'Blimey,' said Trish, 'that's your policeman chum, right?'

'It certainly is,' said Mel, grinning at her mother. 'Keith Penrose and Mum are the major crime-busting team of West Cornwall.'

'Rubbish,' Felicity insisted. 'It was so kind of him to remember my birthday. I wonder how his daughter is doing, I've been meaning to ring him.'

'What's wrong with his daughter?' Trish asked.

'She has cancer,' Felicity said. 'Poor Inspector

10

Penrose, he just adores that girl. I must get in touch with him to see how things are.'

The birthday lunch took place at the Island Hotel. It remained a wonderful day and the adults sat at a table outside while the boys roared around on the grass, running down to the beach now and again and coming back with all manner of treasures. It was a very relaxed affair with just her immediate family around her and exactly what Felicity had wanted. There had been much talk of a big party perhaps back in Oxford, Felicity's hometown, but she had not wanted a fuss – this was perfect. She scrutinised the assembled company under the rim of the battered old straw hat of which she was eccentrically fond. Mel, her daughter, was kicking a football around with Sam and Harry – blonde, long legged, tanned, gorgeous – she seemed oblivious of the stares she was receiving from fellow male diners. That was one of Mel's charms, Felicity thought, she was genuinely and totally unaware of how good-looking she was and that made her even more attractive. The boys were wild with excitement, they adored their aunt, and the football game seemed to involve a lot of collapsing on the ground, tickling and laughing.

Her daughter-in-law, Trish, sat beside her smiling benevolently at the antics. Felicity and Charlie had not been at all sure about Trish when Jamie had first brought her home. The couple had met while Trish was on her gap year, doing the almost obligatory trip around Europe enjoyed by so many young Australians. She was a big girl, tall and broad, not fat but big boned, healthy, hearty and very loud. She seemed to dominate Jamie physically, as well as being so self-confident in contrast to his self-effacing shyness. Her laugh alone had made Charlie wince, Felicity remembered with a smile. For all that, Trish had a good heart – she was sensible, practical, down to earth and clearly adored their son. He was lucky to have her, they all were and just as she had built up Jamie's confidence, Trish herself had mellowed. Felicity turned her attention to Jamie. He was sitting relaxed in his chair toying with a glass of wine, his eyes fixed on the far horizon, apparently oblivious of all that was going on around him – ever the dreamer she thought. He had inherited her physique and so was small and slim, his fair hair was already receding; he looked older than his years. Her heart lurched at the memory of Jamie, the little boy, afraid of everything at school – bullied, shy, dyslexic, terrified of everything and everyone – and how by sheer luck they had discovered his aptitude for IT. He ran his own IT consultancy business now with Trish making sure the practical side of the business ran smoothly – invoices sent out, bills paid. Jamie so loved his work, that left to his own devices, he would have happily done it for nothing. As it was, thanks to Trish, they were comfortably off, living in a charming farmhouse with their two little boys. If Mel would just settle down,

Felicity thought, her parental duties would be all but accomplished.

With the soft enchanting light so special to Scilly, the warmth, the sunshine, the wine, her family around her, Felicity knew she should feel happy and she did, but there was a shadow hovering in the back of her mind. Charlie as always was the spectre at the feast. She remembered his own fiftieth birthday party five years before. Charlie's birthday was in early January and they had celebrated both this and the dawn of a new millennium with a huge party at home, a marquee covering nearly the whole garden, blow heaters working all day to try and take off the worst of the January chill. She had done the catering herself and it had been hard work. Mel was notoriously undomesticated and at university anyway, Trish was about to produce Harry and was coping with Sam who was a truly terrible two at the time. She had been exhausted but not so much as to spoil the pleasure of seeing how much Charlie enjoyed his party – the centre of attention surrounded by all his best friends and work colleagues. Who would have thought, seeing him that evening, that within two years he would be dead, killed because of a dark secret he had carried through all the years of their marriage. It was his duplicity, which still made her sad. It tainted everything, every memory. Here she was fifty, her past so coloured by deception, too young to spend the rest of her life alone, too old to start again with a new partner. This was not a view shared by her Oxford friends who were always embarrassingly trying to introduce her to any stray unattached male who crossed their paths. She couldn't imagine starting again – how could she ever trust another man for a start. If she couldn't trust Charlie, the companion of her whole adult life, the father of her children, who could she trust?

'Granny, Granny, watch me.' Harry aimed a huge kick at the football, missed completely and fell over. Everyone laughed, including Harry, happy to be the clown. Sam would have been mortified, would have hated to be laughed at, to be seen as having messed up. Extraordinary how different the boys were, like her own children. It never failed to amaze Felicity that despite the same basic ingredients and the same upbringing, siblings could be so different.

'I'm just going to pop to the loo,' Felicity murmured to Trish. She stood up and began climbing up the steps leading to the hotel terrace.

A man walking towards her, coming suddenly out of the shadows by the hedge, which bordered the terrace made her jump. He was in a hurry, apparently, heading across the grass towards the footballers and the beach. He was at once familiar. As he passed her, she instinctively called after him. 'Hugo!'

For a split second the figure seemed to freeze and then without looking back, strode off at great speed across the lawn. Felicity stared after him. How ridiculous, what on earth had made Felicity think the man was Hugo Irving? From his departing back

Felicity could see he was one of those fifty-something year olds who sported a ponytail – a grey wispy one, very sad. He was also wearing a T-shirt and cargo pants far more suited to someone less than half his age. What on earth had possessed her to think he was Hugo Irving? Apart from anything else, poor Hugo was dead.

2

'Would that be Chief Inspector Penrose?' The emphasis was on the word Chief.

Keith recognised the voice immediately and smiled. Barely visible behind the piles of papers on his desk, he swivelled his chair away from them and gazed out of the window to the car park below.

'Mrs Paradise, how nice to hear from you, how are you?'

'Well, rather in awe, Chief Inspector. Are you too smart to talk to me these days?'

'I always have time for you, you know that, though please tell me you haven't rung with some awful mystery for me to unravel.'

'I have absolutely no ulterior motive for the call,' said Felicity, smiling too. 'I just wanted to thank you for the birthday card and was wondering whether you could spare time for a quick lunch so that I could offer my congratulations on your promotion.'

'When had you in mind?' Keith asked.

'I suppose today would be no good, would it? I have to be in Truro for a dental appointment.'

Keith considered. 'I am free but it would have to be a quick one – early, say about twelve-thirty?'

They met in the upstairs café of Lemon Street Market, a cheerful place surrounded by art, where light streamed in through the glass roof, giving the illusion of sunshine, even on a dull day. Keith was already waiting for her and he stood up as she approached the table. There was a moment's awkwardness. They had been through too much together, shared too many intimacies in their respective lives, to shake hands and yet there was a formality to their relationship that somehow made it inappropriate for them to kiss or embrace. They stood smiling happily, clearly delighted to see one another, but slightly bashful, awkward, like a couple of teenagers.

'Sit down, please do sit down,' Keith fussed. 'How are you? I must say your half-century seems to agree with you.'

And indeed it did. Her blonde hair, lightly streaked now with grey, shone with health in a short bob, her skin was clear and surprisingly youthful-looking. She was very slim and her movements were quick and lithe, her dress as always, colourful and slightly eccentric – canary yellow trousers, topped by a big red T-shirt and a stripy scarf.

'I'm good,' she admitted, 'though still coming to terms with the significant birthday. I can't believe I'm so ancient, I just don't know where the years have gone.'

'Fifty is the new thirty,' said Keith, firmly.

'Well thank you for that, Chief Inspector,' Felicity said with a grin, 'and congratulations again on your promotion – richly deserved.'

They ordered a glass of wine and a plate of pasta. 'Now tell me about Carly,' said Felicity, suddenly serious. 'How is she?'

'In remission,' said Keith, 'her hair has grown back and she has started training to be a physio. She goes for check-ups every month but so far so good. She is being very positive, but ...,' a shadow crossed his face.

'But what?' Felicity asked.

He was silent for a moment, clearly searching for a way to express himself. 'There are four of us in the house now,' he said. 'My wife Barbara, my daughter Carly, me ... and the cancer – it's always there, just below the surface. On the days she goes into hospital for her check-up, we're all back in the nightmare of it until she comes home. We can't seem to move on from it, or at least, maybe it's just me who can't and I'm still so very angry.'

'Angry?' Felicity asked.

'Angry that Carly has cancer and not me. Look at me – fifty-seven, I've had my life, my career, marriage and children. Heaven knows I don't want cancer but it should be me suffering not Carly, she hasn't even begun to live yet.'

Felicity was silent for a moment, trying to imagine what it would be like if Mel had been diagnosed with cancer, as Carly had been two years before. Yes, she would feel exactly the same. She smiled at him. 'I would feel exactly as you do in the same circumstances, if it was Mel, but the fact is you must try not to let it colour your lives, you do have to move forward, put it behind you, as much for Carly as for you and your wife.'

'I think Carly is doing just that,' Keith said, 'it's just Barbara and I who are still drowning in the horror of it all.'

'It's because we always want the best for our children,' said Felicity, 'and anything less than the best eats away at us.'

Their meal arrived. 'On a more cheerful note, how was Scilly?' Keith asked.

'Wonderful,' said Felicity. 'It was lovely to have the family all together and I had a great birthday, perfect weather.'

'I always want to have a Cornish holiday,' said Keith. 'The trouble is summer is the one time of year I can never get away – with the population explosion in season, comes trouble. It drives Barbara mad.'

'You haven't a big case on at the moment, have you?' Felicity asked.

Keith shook his head. 'No, in fact, this afternoon I'm filling my time by reviewing an old one. I'm going over to St Ives to talk to Miles Irving, Sir Hugo Irving's son.'

'Why?' Felicity asked, sharply. 'Has something happened? Has Hugo been found?'

'No, no,' said Keith, shaking his head. 'Quite the contrary, we're talking through the mechanics of how to start the proceedings to recognise he is dead.'

Felicity put down her fork and frowned at him. 'Go on,' she said.

Keith looked up, met her eye and grimaced. 'Oh no,' he mocked, 'don't tell me you've a theory on Hugo. Let me guess, you and your second sight, you've seen him, you know what happened to him, he's alive and well and living with a gorgeous girl half his age on a Caribbean island.'

Felicity gave a slightly nervous laugh. 'You and your imagination, Chief Inspector, just tell me what you know – humour me.'

'That's easily done,' said Keith, cheerfully, 'absolutely nothing. Sir Hugo Irving simply disappeared that day off Porthmeor beach. There were no witnesses – no one saw him go into the sea and no one saw him come out. The only 'person' who seemed convinced that there had been an accident was a mongrel dog, called Archie, who sadly cannot justify his opinion.' He smiled and then grew serious. 'We've checked everything. In many respects, as you know, he could be rather brash, over the top, something of a bully, but he appears to have been exactly as we saw him – a clever man good at making money, with no skeletons in his cupboard, no scandals, no scams. There was no need for dodgy dealings, he was too wealthy; wealth achieved by legitimate means. He had a long and seemingly happy marriage, he was the only child of humble but apparently devoted parents. His doctor confirms that he had recently undergone a full medical and that he was in good health. The Irvings have another holiday home on Crete. We've checked that out, there has been no sign of him, there is no sign of him anywhere. Missing presumed dead, except that ...' Keith paused.

'Except that what?' Felicity asked.

Keith shook his head. 'I just don't believe it, for some reason I can't explain, I don't believe he drowned.'

'Really Chief Inspector, that's not like you, it's normally me who has the crazy notions.'

Keith smiled. 'This is true,' he acknowledged. 'Look, let me run this past you. It was a very calm day. There were a few decent sets coming in, apparently, but on the whole, the surf was pretty insignificant. Sir Hugo had surfed most of his life. Long before he made his millions, he and his family used to come on holiday to St Ives. He knew Porthmeor, he understood the dangers of rip currents, not that there was one that day.'

'He could have had a heart attack or a stroke, couldn't he?' said Felicity. 'How old was he?'

'Sixty-one – yes easily, he was the prime age for it, but if he had then his body should have been found.'

'You found the surfboard.'

'Yes,' said Keith, 'and there was no question that it was his board and it had been smashed.'

'Well, that explains it, surely, he must have struck a rock,' said Felicity, 'or been run down by a boat, I suppose.'

'It is very hard to break those fibreglass surfboards. It looked …' he hesitated,

'What?' Felicity asked.

'Well, kind of theatrical to me. It was like the broken surfboard was a prop. The stage was set for Sir Hugo to drown and here was the proof, conveniently provided, case closed before it was hardly opened.'

Felicity toyed with her cooling pasta. 'You're not going to like what I have to say,' she said, 'or then again, maybe you are. I wasn't going to mention it but since you've raised doubts then I have to admit I thought I saw him on Tresco last week.'

'Saw who?' Keith frowned.

'Sir Hugo, of course, who do you think?'

'What – and you didn't ring me?'

'I didn't ring you, Chief Inspector, because I didn't want to be ridiculed,' she smiled, trying to lighten the mood. 'We've been here so many times before. I ring you up with some hair-brained notion and you tell me I'm talking a load of rubbish. So, I thought I saw him but decided it was quite impossible so, for once in my life, practised some degree of restraint, and did … nothing.'

'So why are you telling me now?' Keith asked.

'Because, as I've just said, you've expressed

doubts as to his disappearance. I don't want to be thrown into a dungeon for withholding information.'

It was Keith's turn to smile. 'Tell me exactly what happened,' he said.

'We were having lunch at the Island Hotel,'

'Lucky you!'

'It was my birthday, remember. I was on my way into the hotel to go to the loo and I was walking up the steps onto the terrace when I saw him. I didn't think, I just called out "Hugo" and for a moment I thought he hesitated and then he walked on. He had a ponytail, a none too clean T-shirt and he was wearing cargo pants.'

'What?' Keith choked over his wine.

'Yes, I know, it does sound ridiculous, Sir Hugo Irving sporting a ponytail.'

'So what on earth made you think it was him?'

'I saw his features in profile, just for a moment, that and the way he walked. You know how he walks, he has a very straight back, shoulders thrown back, almost strutting. It was that as much as his profile that made me think it was him.'

'And the fact that he hesitated when you called his name,' Keith said.

'Yes, that too.'

'And you really weren't going to tell me?'

Felicity relented. 'Even if you hadn't mentioned Sir Hugo, I probably would have done, I'll admit.'

'I never thought I'd find myself asking this question,' Keith had the good sense to look a little bashful, 'but what were your feelings about the encounter? Did you believe it was Sir Hugo?'

'If you're asking whether I had a moment of second sight, the answer is no. I had no particular feelings one way or the other, which is why I suppose I've hesitated to get in touch with you. All I can say is that, as you can imagine, on my birthday, surrounded by my family, Sir Hugo Irving hadn't even crossed my mind. I wasn't thinking about him in any way so the chance encounter was not something I could have possibly expected or dreamed up. It came right out of the blue.'

'Shall we order coffee?' Felicity nodded. Keith leant back on his chair. 'So why would he risk it?'

'Risk what?' Felicity asked.

'Coming back to Cornwall. Just supposing for a moment that his death was no accident, but a deliberate attempt to run away, why would he risk coming back to Scilly where someone such as you could recognise him? If you were going to run away and you had Sir Hugo's resources, then presumably you would do it properly and go somewhere no one would ever find you and start a new life that was absolutely untraceable.'

'Is that still possible in today's world?'

'Not for most of us, no,' said Keith, 'but if you've got enough money, yes, it is still possible.'

'Presumably you've checked his bank accounts and all that sort of thing?'

'There are absolutely no irregularities, no big

24

withdrawals, nothing like that, but, of course, if this is something he has been planning for a while, he could have been salting money away in some offshore account for years and we'd be none the wiser.'

'I suppose not,' said Felicity, thoughtfully. 'Maybe he had some unfinished business in Cornwall and thought Tresco was a safe place to come. After all, in July most of the visitors are from up-country. It was just bad luck we'd chosen to spend my birthday weekend there.'

'Did you like him?' Keith asked, thoughtfully.

'I hardly knew him,' said Felicity. 'The only times we ever met was at our bi-annual hospice meetings, oh, and the Christmas ball of course.'

'Didn't you dance with him last Christmas, as I recall?'

'I did, yes and in answer to your question, no I didn't like him. He was a very charismatic man of course, and I liked his commitment to the hospice, but I didn't like the feeling that everything had to be done his way.'

'Remember he lost a child,' Keith said. 'Miles is his only surviving child, but there was a daughter. She was diagnosed with leukaemia at two and died at five.'

'I know, it's awful, poor people, no amount of money can protect you from that situation,' said Felicity. 'Tell me now, did you like him?'

Keith sighed. 'Yes I suppose I did but I suspect I was rather caught up in the web of his charm. I liked the way he had time for a small Cornish charity. Even though he had a personal reason to be involved, it did him credit that he spent so much time on our small project.'

'He was also very gracious and encouraging, wasn't he?' said Felicity. 'He made you feel you were doing a good job. He had huge charm.'

Keith nodded. 'It's one of the things that has come out since his disappearance. His staff adored him, all of them, we couldn't find anyone prepared to dish the dirt.'

'So if they all adored him so much, presumably they'd have been prepared to cover up for him?' Felicity suggested. 'Absolute loyalty like that could be hiding something, I suppose.'

Keith shrugged. 'I don't know, I've been round it so many times – I just feel he is still alive.' He gave a short laugh. 'Hell, I really am starting to sound like you.'

'Are you going to tell Miles about my sighting?' Felicity asked after a moment.

'I don't know,' Keith admitted, 'it's a difficult call. He appears to be a surprisingly unsophisticated lad, quite young for his age and he is only eighteen. I understand he is the centre of his parents' world. They never thought they would have children after their daughter died and then Miles arrived when they were in their forties. I suspect he's been wrapped in cotton wool for most of his childhood and he seems somewhat unworldly. I imagine he is very upset by his father's disappearance.'

'In which case,' said Felicity, 'I think you should say nothing. It was such a fleeting thing, I was probably imagining it.'

'You – imagining something, Mrs Paradise, hardly likely, I would have thought.' His smile was annoyingly patronising.

'Sarcasm does not suit you, Chief Inspector,' Felicity replied tartly.

3

Sergeant Jack Curnow swore under his breath as their car ground to a halt behind a long queue of traffic waiting to clear Chiverton roundabout from the Truro direction.

'It's not even the rush hour,' he grumbled. 'Cornwall's getting like everywhere else, too many cars.' He glanced at his boss, sitting in the passenger seat beside him. 'I'm sorry, sir, it's my fault we left late. Do you want me to put up the siren?'

Chief Inspector Keith Penrose shook his head. 'No need, Jack,' he said, 'we'll be through this lot in ten minutes and we'll still have half an hour to get to St Ives, we've plenty of time. I don't expect young Miles Irving will mind if we're a few minutes late in any event. He's probably hooked up with some friends while he's down here and just happy to have got away. They say Lady Irving is taking her husband's disappearance very hard.'

'It's the uncertainty, I expect,' said Jack, edging the car forward at a snail's pace, 'not that I know anything about women – or so I'm told.'

Keith glanced at him, amused. 'Are you in trouble at home again, Jack?'

'When am I ever not?' Jack said, ruefully.

Keith studied his sergeant's profile in silence for a moment. Jack looked strained, his face had lost some of its youthful roundness, he certainly did not appear to be a happy man.

Jack's family, like Keith's own, were farmers. They had farmed out on the Lizard for generations. In the early days of working together, before Jack had married, Keith had visited his family home on a several occasions. It was a modest little farmhouse on an exposed piece of land close to the cliff edge but somehow the Curnows had managed to eke out a living for themselves, Jack and his four siblings. They were a cheerful family, calm and accepting of life's hardships with resignation and good humour. Keith remembered visiting them during the foot and mouth epidemic. With a small dairy herd the family were worried, naturally, but there was a laid back fatalism about them – what would be, would be. There was no point worrying about it until the worst happened and mercifully, in their case, it never did. Seeing Jack, so tense now, concerned Keith.

'What's up then, Jack?'

'Oh the usual,' said Jack. 'Now Maggie is pregnant she wants me around all the time. I can't understand it. Mum and my sisters are never happier than when they can get their men out of the front door. I've tried explaining to her about police work but she just doesn't want to know, she just gets upset and tearful, I hate that.'

'Hormones,' said Keith, glumly, 'they go mad during pregnancy. I expect that's what's causing the trouble.'

'I don't think so,' said Jack, 'she was like it before she was even pregnant, it's just worse now,' he hesitated. 'She wants me to leave the Force, you know?'

'You're not going to, Jack, are you? You're made for police work.'

'No, I'm not,' said Jack. 'What other kind of job could I get down here and I'm not leaving Cornwall. She wants me to go up-country to be near her folks, but I won't do it.'

'I suppose,' said Keith, with a heavy heart, 'we could organise you a transfer, if that's what you want.'

'It's not what I want,' said Jack. 'I belong down here, this is my home.'

'Maybe she feels the same about up-country,' Keith ventured.

Jack shook his head vehemently. 'Can't do, her parents have lived all over. I told her when I proposed I would always have to live in Cornwall. She was fine about it then, now …' he sighed heavily, 'you're lucky Mrs Penrose is Cornish.' Jack added as an afterthought.

'Yes, I suppose I am,' Keith admitted, 'though it wasn't all plain sailing for me either. Barbara's parents didn't think I was good enough for her and they were probably right too.'

'Really?' Jack glanced at his boss, surprised.

'Yes,' said Keith. 'Her family lived up Bodmin way. Barbara's father was in the army and her mother was very bright, something of an intellectual …' he hesitated, 'I suppose if you were being unkind, you'd say an intellectual snob. She had been to university, to Cambridge, at a time when very few women did so. I guess she was expecting great things of Barbara – certainly not marrying the local PC, which is what I was at the time.'

'But you've done alright for yourself, sir, if you don't mind my saying so.'

Keith laughed. 'I don't mind you saying so, Jack. No, it has turned out alright, but like your Maggie, Barbara has always considered the Force to be the other woman in my life. She knows the job has to come first but she still resents it. She has just learnt to live with it, I suppose, as your Maggie will have to do.'

'Or leave me,' said Jack, 'that's what she's threatened to do.'

'She won't now there is a baby on the way,' said Keith, with more conviction then he felt, 'don't worry she will settle down.'

The traffic cleared and the two men lapsed into a companionable silence as Jack joined the A30 and headed for St Ives. Keith thought back through the mists of time to when his children, Billy and Carly, were small. It had been hard for Barbara coping with two tiny children with him away so much of the time, coming back all hours, preoccupied. You had to be a certain sort to be a policeman's wife and heaven knows the number of broken marriages within the Force was testament enough to how difficult it was. Would Maggie Curnow stand up to the test? Sadly, with things so difficult so early on in the marriage, he rather doubted it. Yet Barbara was still with him after all these years. Their relationship had been slightly easier of late. When initially Carly had been diagnosed with cancer, he and Barbara had been at each other's throats all the time. It was the stress, the guilt and the sheer bloody misery, he knew that, but sometimes he had just not wanted to go home. Despite the nightmare of the last couple of years – were they basically happy together? He could no longer tell. They were used to each other, they both adored their children but he realised now that they had been very different people with different aspirations when they had married, and those differences had sharpened and intensified over the years. His job was his life and he was now only eight years away from retirement. He couldn't bear to think about what would happen when he was forced to give up.

The Irvings' holiday home was one of the few detached houses in central St Ives, set up above the town with a glorious view of the harbour. It was a secret place, hard to find unless you knew where you were going. Keith had been there once to meet Sir Hugo before a hospice get-together, and Jack was impressed as Keith wove his way down from Barnoon car park, through a series of narrow passageways until they reached the house. They pushed open the garden gate and climbed up on to a sumptuous terrace with views to die for.

'Not bad for a second home,' Jack whispered as they approached the front door.

'Come on, Jack,' said Keith, 'we shouldn't begrudge him – Sir Hugo gave a lot away to charity, you know.'

'Clearly not all of it,' said Jack, with a grin.

They rang the bell and waited, there was no reply. After a few minutes Keith attacked the doorknocker and gave it a vicious pounding, still nothing.

'That's odd,' said Keith, glancing at his watch. 'We said three o'clock and it's after that now.'

'Kids,' said Jack, 'notoriously bad timekeepers.'

'Not this one, I suspect,' Keith said. 'Very correct, very courteous, old fashioned really.'

'You've met him?' Jack asked.

'No, no, I've only spoken to him on the phone but he sounded much older than his years.'

'And you're sure there isn't a mix up and he's expecting to meet you in London?'

'Absolutely not, I'm not completely senile,' said Keith, 'that was the whole point. He was down for the weekend and so it was a good opportunity for us to get together.'

'I'll try round the back,' said Jack, 'perhaps the back door is unlocked.'

With Jack gone, Keith turned his back on the house and gazed out on St Ives Bay laid out below him. The water was glacially still, it looked more like a lake than the sea, the sun beat down on the terrace – it was a real suntrap. He stared over the rooftops, Felicity's cottage had to be one of those roofs. He had enjoyed seeing her today and it amused him that for once it was him creating a mystery where probably there was none. It was a considerable role reversal.

It was strange that Miles wasn't here. He turned back towards the house, staring at it thoughtfully. He realised slowly that all his instincts were telling him something was wrong.

Jack appeared around the side of the house. 'The back door is locked,' he said. 'I tried hammering on that too, but there is no response. There's definitely no one in, sir.'

They peered through the windows. While there appeared to be no one around, the house looked lived-in. On the dining room table there was a bowl of fresh fruit, through the sitting room window they could see a vase of flowers. Someone had either been there or was imminently expected.

'Perhaps he has been held up on the motorway, sir.'

'No, no,' said Keith, 'he was coming down yesterday by train and in any event he has my mobile number. He said he would call me if there was any problem.' Keith was peering through a stained glass panel in the front door and frowned. 'There's something in the hallway – I don't like the look of it,' he said over his shoulder.

Jack joined him and peered through the glass. 'I can't see anything, sir, it's just a shadow, I think.'

'No,' said Keith, 'I don't think so.' He was eyeing the front door, speculatively. It was Georgian, wide, panelled, solid as a rock. 'What's the back door like, Jack?'

'Just a standard wooden door.'

'Not like this one?' Keith asked. Jack shook his head. 'Right, good because we're going to break it down.'

'Are you sure, sir? Isn't that a bit of an over-reaction?' Jack looked appalled.

'Absolutely not,' said Keith firmly, 'something's up.'

'I hope you're right, sir. It hardly seems justified to be breaking into the house just because someone is late for his appointment with you.'

'Oh, stop fussing, you sound like a right old woman,' said Keith, testily, starting round the side of the house.

The back door gave way with surprising ease confronted by the weight of the two men. It was not bolted, and the door lock was old fashioned and fragile. They stood in the kitchen in silence for a moment. All the instincts, which had told Keith something was wrong, became hideously clear. It was the smell, the strange, sickening, metallic smell that could only be blood. He followed his nose out of the kitchen and into the hallway, a narrow dark space, the only light coming from the panel of stained glass in the front door. The shadow he had seen on the floor was not a shadow. It was a body. Groping along the wall he found a switch and turned on the hallway light. It was the body of a young woman, dark hair splayed out across the floor, long luxurious hair. She lay on her side, her arms up about her head, obviously trying to fend off the attack, pointlessly as it turned out. It had been what the papers would describe as a frenzied attack. The victim had suffered multiple stab wounds. There was blood everywhere, on the floor, on the walls. The girl was wearing jeans and a T-shirt, but there was so much blood, it was impossible to tell what colour the T-shirt had been.

'Oh God!' Keith heard Jack gasp behind him and heard him moments later retching in the kitchen. He didn't feel that steady himself. Up-country the Force had to cope with this sort of thing on a regular basis, particularly in inner cities, but although Keith had been involved in several murders over the years, he had never seen anything quite like this. Jack was back beside him, wiping his face with a piece of kitchen roll.

'Sorry, sir.'

'It's alright,' said Keith, putting his hand on his arm, 'alright now?'

'Yes sir,' Jack said none too steadily.

'We'd better check the rest of the house and make sure this is the only one,' said Keith, 'then we'll call in.'

'I'll take upstairs,' said Jack, obviously anxious to get away from the terrible scene before them.

'Right.'

Keith stepped carefully around the body, and edged his way into what turned out to be the sitting room. The fresh flowers stood jauntily on the table where he and Jack had spied them, what seemed a long time ago now. The room was polished, neat, untouched, there was no sign of any disturbance. He carefully retraced his steps, and opened the door opposite into the dining room. It was the mirror of the sitting room, a large pleasant room with a bay window and again the fruit bowl they had seen. He stood staring around him for a moment. It was an old house this, three or four hundred years old – probably, Georgian, certainly older than the Victorian terraces which dominated St Ives. Even now, it had a tranquil atmosphere, and he could well see why the Irvings liked it as a holiday home. In its long history, he wondered if the house had ever witnessed anything like the scene in the hall. He pulled out his mobile phone and with hands that trembled, rung the station. By the time he had finished his call Jack had joined him.

'Nothing up there, sir,' he said.

'Let's go back in the kitchen,' said Keith, 'touch

nothing,' he added, unnecessarily.

In the kitchen there was the same order which was maintained throughout the house. Everything was neat, clean and in its place.

'I wonder who the hell she is?' said Keith. 'There is no bag with her. Did you notice anything upstairs?'

'I don't think anybody has been upstairs. It looked just like, well, like the rest of the house, untouched, in perfect order and there's no luggage. We could check her pockets, I suppose,' he added faintly.

'No,' said Keith. 'We have to let forensics do that. She looks very young,' he added, 'and very different from the Irvings and their friends.'

'In what way?' Jack asked.

'Did you notice her shoes, they're all scuffed, broken almost.'

'You mean she was some sort of vagrant, sir, is that what you're saying?'

'No,' said Keith. 'I'm just saying she was short of money and the Irvings don't move in circles with people who are short of money. She is not one of them, that's all I'm saying.'

'So the big burning question now,' said Jack, 'is … where's Miles?'

'And question two,' said Keith, 'is he responsible for this?'

'He's an obvious candidate,' Jack said, leaning back against the sink looking as though he still needed support.

'Not really,' said Keith, 'you'd hardly make a date with a policeman and then when the policeman turns up, leave your murder victim for him to find. Not a very bright move, I would have thought.'

'No,' Jack agreed.

'On the other hand,' said Keith. 'Whoever did this had a key, the place was locked up.'

'So,' said Jack, 'it either has to be Miles, or staff, friends or family with a key, or ...'

'Or,' Keith interjected, 'Sir Hugo Irving, back from the dead.'

4

By the time Felicity turned off the A30 towards St Ives the local anaesthetic had worn off and her tooth was throbbing with a vengeance. She hated the dentist's more than anything, declaring she would rather have twins than a tooth filling. Just where the road narrowed by Carbis Bay, she heard a great commotion behind her, a police car flashed past her heading towards St Ives, followed shortly afterwards by an ambulance and another police car.

'Very unusual goings on for St Ives', Felicity thought, 'there must have been an accident on the beach.'

She was in a hurry herself to see whether she had received an e-mail from a publisher she had approached. She had submitted a series of flower drawings following her holiday on Tresco. The publisher was producing a book on Cornish growing successes – both the indigenous plants that had flourished the length of the Cornish coast for centuries but also the newer, more exotic, foreign species which were thriving in the mild salty air.

Plants were not normally Felicity's subject, she drew people or animals best, but she had been quite pleased with her work on Tresco and was hoping to be commissioned to do at least a few of the illustrations. She parked at Barnoon Car Park; the police cars and ambulance were already there, the occupants of all the vehicles presumably having disappeared into the maze of little lanes that led down towards the harbour.

'Must be something big going on,' Felicity thought, as she set off for home.

Jericho Cottage had been her home now for three years. It was an upside down house. There were two bedrooms and a bathroom on the ground floor, and on the first floor a kitchen/dining room, a little sitting room and a balcony with glorious views across the harbour. It suited Felicity perfectly and it gave her real pleasure to come home. Orlando was cross. He gave her a ferocious stare and then pretended to ignore her. His ancient digestion now required three tiny meals a day and he liked them on time. Lunch was favoured for two o'clock and it was now nearly four.

'I'm sorry Orlando, I'll get it straight away,' said Felicity flicking on the kettle and searching for a tin of cat food. It was like living with some querulous old person, she thought – no, it is living with some querulous old person. She gave him an affectionate smile and a stroke behind the ear. He pretended not to notice; he was in a deep sulk.

With the cat fed and a mug of tea in hand, Felicity opened her laptop. There was an e-mail from the publisher. With beating heart she opened it and yes, she had been commissioned to do twelve drawings – all the plants in question could be found either on Tresco or in the gardens of St Michael's Mount. It was more than she dared hope for and the money was good, too. It was her first commission from a mainstream publisher and much more exciting than the money was the thought that she was actually being paid as an illustrator. After years of teaching art in school in order to fit her working life around raising a family, it was a very heady sensation to think that this might be the beginning of a whole new career – and at fifty too!

'We'll be rich and famous yet, Orlando,' Felicity assured him. His temper restored by a delicate sufficiency of food, he allowed his ears to be tickled and even bestowed on her the favour of a gentle purr. Outside the sirens started wailing again. What on earth was going on? It sounded more like an inner city on a Saturday night than St Ives.

Felicity made an immediate start the following morning. She decided to visit St Michael's Mount as early as possible before the visitors were out in force. It was an overcast day but warm. She took the back road from town towards Penzance and as she climbed out of the village of Nancledra, below her the sweep of Mount's Bay came into view, dominated by the Mount. It was a view that never failed to arrest her. She glanced at her watch, she was in good time. The Mount Gardens were only open to the public on Thursdays and Fridays and then not until 10.30. She was early and on impulse she pulled off the road into a lay-by and sat in the car for a few minutes drinking in the scene. The sun was starting to filter through the clouds and the sea had turned silver. John of Gaunt's famous words 'Set in a silver sea' touched her mind, England at its best, so very special – 'this sceptred isle'. She turned her attention to the Mount, the great rock towering out of the water with the castle clinging to it and the cottages clustered around the little harbour below. It was so extraordinary, so unique and not for the first time, she speculated on how privileged she was to live in such a beautiful part of the world. After all the trials and tribulations of the last few years, it seemed as if she was truly blessed. With a sigh of pure pleasure, she slipped the car into gear and begun the long descent to the sea.

She parked the car in Marazion and just had time to walk across the Causeway before the tide came in. It would mean coming back from the Mount by boat. The clouds were really lifting now and shafts of light backlit the Mount dramatically, it was more like a stage set than real life and Felicity was very tempted to abandon all thoughts of drawing plants and make her subject the Mount instead, as so many artists had before her through the centuries. She enjoyed the walk across the causeway. Water was starting to lap the edge of the cobbles so she did not dawdle. Already there were a surprising number of people about so she was anxious to get into the gardens before there were too many visitors.

She spent a pleasant morning sketching. One or two of her sketches really quite pleased her and she could see them being worked up into the kind of illustration she felt the publishers wanted. She would have to come back of course, but it was a start. Mid-morning she stopped for cup of coffee and then pressed on. By now people were everywhere and after a while became quite intrusive, asking what she was doing and why. It was always the same with art. You only had to set up an easel or sit on a rock with a sketchpad, as she was doing now, and it seemed to make you public property. People felt free to come up and look over your shoulder and make comments about what you were doing in a way they would never do if you were simply sitting reading a book. In most respects, Felicity was a sociable outgoing person but not where her art was concerned, she felt embarrassed, a fraud, she lacked confidence. As soon as somebody started looking at her work she had an overwhelming desire to snap shut the sketchbook and run away. By early afternoon, she could stand the public interest no longer and made her way to the harbour. There was a long queue for the boats but that was no problem, she was in no hurry, and the little harbour was enchanting. The sun was out in force now, the sea sparkling, a stiff breeze sent wispy clouds scudding across the sky, it was exhilarating.

Immediately ahead of Felicity in the queue were a man and a dog. The dog gave her a kindly look and she bent down to pat him. It was rather an odd looking creature with an excessively curly coat and she was dimly aware of having seen him before somewhere.

'Archie can never have too much fuss.' The man addressing her was a tall, slightly stooped figure with the same kindly expression as his dog. He was a man in his late sixties, early seventies and he too was oddly familiar.

'Do you come from St Ives?' Felicity asked.

'Yes we do,' the man held out a hand. 'I'm Henry Sinclair and this is Archie.'

'Hello Archie,' said Felicity. 'My name is Felicity Paradise. I live in St Ives too. I thought I had seen you two about.'

'It's not me you will have remembered,' said Henry, with a smile, 'it's Archie. It's always been the case. He is the more, how shall I put it, striking of the pair of us and he was something of a celebrity back in March.'

'Of course,' said Felicity, 'that's why I know you. This is the dog who spotted that Sir Hugo Irving was missing. You really are a celebrity, Archie.' Archie thumped his tail in agreement.

'Absolutely,' Henry agreed.

They had reached the front of the queue and became involved in boarding a boat. During the boarding they became separated and it wasn't until they reached the mainland that they joined forces again.

'Is your car here?' Felicity asked.

'No,' said Henry, 'I don't drive anymore. We were going to walk into Penzance and catch a train.'

'Why don't I give you a lift back to St Ives?'

Henry looked doubtfully at Archie. 'You sure you want Archie in your car, he has very sandy paws?'

'I'm not at all bothered,' said Felicity, 'and you'll understand why when you see the state of my car.'

'Then we'd both be delighted to accept,' said Henry.

They were soon in the car with Archie stretched out on the back seat on an old rug looking very pleased with himself.

'Anyway as it has turned out, Archie appears to have uncovered only the tip of the iceberg,' said Henry, conversationally.

'How do you mean?' Felicity asked.

'You heard about the terrible business last night, didn't you?'

'What terrible business?' Felicity asked.

'The police found the body of a young woman at the Irvings' holiday home.'

'A dead body?' Felicity asked.

'Yes,' said Henry, 'a very dead body according to a chum of mine, who knows someone in the Force.

She had been brutally stabbed, apparently. Poor girl – it's hardly the sort of thing that normally happens in St Ives.'

'How terrible,' said Felicity, 'who was she?'

'No idea. The reporting was a bit sketchy on the news last night but the town is buzzing with it. I'm surprised you haven't heard anything about it.'

'I left home early this morning,' said Felicity, 'and last night I was busy working. I suppose that's what all the sirens were about?'

'Yes,' said Henry. 'It didn't sound like our little town at all yesterday, did it? It's the seagulls who are normally our noisiest feature.'

'Yes,' said Felicity, with a smile. 'I thought the same. How simply awful, I wonder who on earth this woman can be?' She remembered suddenly that Keith had been going to meet Miles Irving at the house. It must have been he who discovered the body. 'Did they say on the news who was in charge of the case?' Felicity asked.

'Probably, I can't remember the name but no doubt some Inspector from Truro or St Austell I suppose.'

'Chief Inspector Penrose?' Felicity asked.

'Sounds familiar but I can't be sure.'

'What about the son?' Felicity asked.

'The son?' said Henry, frowning.

'Yes, Miles Irving.'

'There was no mention of him at all on the news. I expect he's up in London with his mother.'

For a moment Felicity was tempted to tell Henry what she knew of the case but she was conscious that now things had suddenly become so serious, she should not be admitting to having gossiped about Sir Hugo Irving with the Chief Inspector in charge.

'No doubt we'll get an update on 'Spotlight' tonight but in the meantime the town is crawling with police, asking questions, checking if anybody has seen anything. One way or another that family have certainly had a major impact on the town this year,' Henry said sagely.

Having parked the car and parted company with Henry and Archie, promising to meet again soon, instead of heading home, Felicity took the steep steps down into Virgin Street and to Cormorant Cottage in search of Annie Trethewey. Annie had been Felicity's landlady before she had a home of her own in St Ives and had remained a firm friend. As usual Annie was busy at the Aga.

'There you are my girl,' she said. 'I'm making a few drop scones, you're just in time. I'll put the kettle on.'

Felicity who had missed lunch completely made absolutely no attempt to argue and in any event, Annie's drop scones were to die for. She sat down at the kitchen table.

'How are you, Annie?'

Annie turned and smiled at her. Annie was

seventy-eight now, a tiny frail figure yet still bursting with energy and enthusiasm. She always made Felicity feel lazy and inactive by comparison.

'Never better, my girl and how are you, you're looking bonny, seems you've caught the sun.'

'I was on the Mount sketching. I'm very excited, I've been commissioned to do twelve paintings of indigenous plants for a big publisher. They're paying lots of money, I can't believe it.'

'No more than you deserve, my bird, you draw a lovely picture.' Annie turned back to the Aga and flipped over the scones on the griddle. 'So what can I do for you?' she asked conversationally.

'What makes you think you can do anything for me?' Felicity asked.

'Because, my bird, you only come here when you want something.'

'Annie, that is so untrue,' said Felicity indignantly, 'though I must admit I'm here for a gossip. What can you tell me about this poor woman who was murdered yesterday.'

Annie expertly slipped the scones onto a plate and put a pat of butter and a pot of strawberry jam on the table.

'Well,' she said, 'what a thing to happen in St Ives! Help yourself, lovely, while they're hot. The tea will be ready dreckly.'

Felicity helped herself and waited. She knew it would not be long before Annie divulged her story, but she needed to do it in her own time.

Annie silently poured two cups of tea from the pot, refilled it, placed it on the Aga, fetched a tea cosy from the cupboard and only then came and sat at the table, ready to begin.

'My friend Jenny Stevens cleans for the Irvings,' Annie said, importantly. 'She was there all day at the house, not yesterday, the day before the murder. She was getting the house ready for young Miles who was coming down to stay for a few days. She said nobody had been there since Sir Hugo disappeared so she gave the place a good going over and put in some groceries for the boy and made up his bed. There was no one about then, not a sign of a soul.'

'Inspector Penrose, sorry, Chief Inspector Penrose was due to meet Miles at the house yesterday afternoon.'

'Was he now?' said Annie. 'How do you know a thing like that? Oh, silly question, you and Inspector Penrose tell each other everything.' She grinned, slyly.

'Actually,' said Felicity, defensively 'I had lunch with him yesterday. We had to have an early lunch because he was coming here to talk to Miles. He was going to give him some advice as to how to proceed now it is fairly clear his father is dead.'

'So it must have been your Inspector who discovered the body?'

'I imagine so,' said Felicity.

'Terrible state, apparently, blood everywhere, what a thing, poor girl.' Annie poured more tea.

'So what about Miles?'

'Well,' said Annie, 'according to Jenny, he never showed up. He was due in the night before the murder was discovered, the same day she had been cleaning, but he never arrived. She lives just down from the house and she went up to check about ten o'clock to see if he was here and needed anything. He's only eighteen you know, and I think she is quite fond of the boy, known him since he was little. There was no one there so she just presumed he had missed his train and was coming in the morning, thought no more about it. Now, of course, poor Jenny is all of a jitter. She reckons she could have bumped straight into the murderer, going out that time of night.'

'Do they know when the girl was killed?' Felicity asked.

'Not been reported yet,' Annie said, 'but certainly some time after Jenny's visit. She said she watched the headlines on the ten o'clock news and then went up to the house so she was probably there about ten past ten and certainly there was nobody about then. She has a key of course and let herself in the front door. The body was found in the hall apparently so she could hardly have missed it. The murder must have happened the following day I suppose – at any rate sometime after Jenny leaving and before your Inspector arrived. A terrible business, terrible. I expect your Inspector will have something to say about it this evening on the news. Are you going to help him solve this case too?'

'Stop it, Annie,' said Felicity, firmly. 'When I became involved in his cases in the past, it was because I was personally involved, too – this one is absolutely nothing to do with me though I did know Sir Hugo Irving vaguely.'

'There you go,' said Annie, with a grin, 'you're already in the thick of it.'

'He wasn't a friend or anything, Annie, I just saw him occasionally at a committee we both sat on – you know, the children's hospice thing I'm involved in.'

'I heard he was a big man for his charities, that's nice. A lot of rich men are only rich because they hang on to their money. Have another scone, my bird, you look too thin.'

'Oh, I do so wish I was,' said Felicity. 'I've put on so much weight since I started living down here. I blame you entirely.'

'You were all skin and bone when you arrived, you look much better now,' Annie said, firmly. 'Anyway, no doubt, your inspector will be in touch with you as soon as he needs your help.'

'Don't be silly, Annie,' said Felicity, 'there is absolutely nothing for him to get in touch with me about.'

'Don't you have one of your little feelings about what happened to Sir Hugo?'

'Absolutely none,' said Felicity, 'though strangely enough …' Felicity then told Annie all about her alleged sighting on Tresco.

'There you are,' said Annie, triumphantly. 'You

are involved already. That man can't solve a big crime like this without your help, I'm sure of it.'

At six o'clock Felicity was in front of her television, waiting impatiently for the national news to finish. Sure enough Spotlight was dominated by the murder in St Ives and Keith made a statement to a reporter, the main thrust being an appeal to the public to come forward if they had seen anything suspicious.

'It's a small town, St Ives. I know now the season is on us, with so many visitors around, it is difficult to spot anything unusual and out of the ordinary but think carefully. Someone must have seen something that could be helpful to us. Please come forward.' He quoted a number promising, as usual, that any information would be treated confidentially.

'Was any member of the family living in the house at the time?' the reporter asked.

'The son of the family, Miles Irving, was supposed to be coming down to Cornwall the day of the murder but it appears he never arrived.'

'Really,' said the reporter, 'so is he a suspect, Chief Inspector?'

'Not at the moment,' Keith said, evenly, 'until forensics have finished their job we don't know who we are looking for although, of course, we have leads.'

'And where is Miles Irving now?' The reporter asked.

Keith looked straight into the camera. 'Well that is the strange part,' he admitted, 'like his father he seems to have completely disappeared!'

A spell of bad weather had halted the advancement of Felicity's illustrations – that and a persistent queasy feeling following the news of the murder in the Irvings' house. Although not directly involved in any way, her thoughts rarely strayed from the horrible incident and it was several days before both the weather and her mood lightened sufficiently to enable her to tramp across the causeway towards the Mount again, this time with her easel and paints strapped to her back. She was good at sketching from memory, shapes she could do, but colours, particularly subtle ones, she needed to be there in situ to get them right. With a bit of luck she would get a couple of hours' painting in before the visitors arrived in force. Her mobile rang.

'Drat,' she thought, not wanting any distractions.

'Hi Mum, are you OK?' It was her son, Jamie.

'Yes, of course I'm OK, Jamie, why wouldn't I be?'

'Well, this murder and everything.'

'No one has tried to murder me,' said Felicity, 'at least not so I'd noticed.' She hesitated, 'Sorry, that sounded a bit flip – poor girl, it is dreadful.'

'It sounds ghastly,' said Jamie, 'and your Chief Inspector is in charge I see.'

'I wish everybody would stop calling him my

Chief Inspector,' said Felicity.

'So are you involved in this case?' Jamie asked, ignoring her.

'No and I wish everybody would stop asking me that as well. It really is nothing to do with me.'

'What about the Greshams, you helped him with that?'

'But that was something to do with me,' said Felicity, 'as well you know. The only connection I have with the Irvings is that they have a holiday house in the town in which I live – oh, I have met Sir Hugo a few times at committee meetings and danced with him once and most important of all, Annie knows their cleaning lady.'

Jamie laughed. 'Well that clinches it, Mum, you're up to your neck in it.'

'How are the boys and Trish?' Felicity asked, anxious to change the subject.

'Perfect. We loved our holiday with you and they're missing you frightfully. We thought maybe we might pop down at the end of August, about the time most people are leaving, just after the bank holiday. Do you think we could cram into your cottage?'

'Of course you could but what about the boys, shouldn't they be going back to school then?'

'Ever the school ma'am,' said Jamie, 'it won't hurt them to miss the first few days of school, they're only young.'

'New academic year, new classes, new form teacher,' Felicity said, firmly.

'The school is not that great actually, Mum, it really doesn't matter what they miss. In any event, me and Trish are thinking of home schooling them.'

'Are you, isn't that a bit rash?'

'Why?' Jamie asked.

'Well, you know, missing out on friends, sport, that sort of thing.'

'There are all sorts of ways around that but, hey, we'll tell you all about it when we come down. Are you around early September?'

'I'm always around,' said Felicity. 'I know it's very boring of me, but living here, I never really want to go anywhere else.'

At the same moment that Felicity was talking to her son on the Causeway, Chief Inspector Keith Penrose was sitting at his desk. He had been there since just after seven having travelled down on the sleeper overnight. He had taken the train up to London the previous day on the 5.48 am from Truro and had slept hardly at all on the sleeper on the way back and so was now feeling dreadful. He hadn't been home, fearing a wearing interrogation from Barbara. He kept some shaving gear and a clean shirt permanently at the office and so he had dealt with all his ablutions and was now deep in thought. He had spent most of the previous afternoon with Bettine Irving, wife to Hugo, mother to Miles, both of whom apparently had disappeared off the face of the earth.

Bettine was an elegant woman of aristocratic bearing, and it was hard to imagine her married to Hugo. He in the best traditions of a self-made man was the son of a miner from West Yorkshire. Bettine, by contrast, was the daughter of a peer, raised in Wiltshire, her childhood absorbed by boarding school and the Pony Club. She had been gracious and charming with him, despite the fact that she was obviously almost out of her mind with worry. She had found him a comfortable chair, organised a cup of coffee – the perfect hostess despite everything. The Irving house was sumptuous, a huge end of terrace in a fashionable Notting Hill street. It was the kind of house that if it had been divided into flats would have still provided a substantial and wonderful home on each floor, but Sir Hugo Irving owned the lot. The drawing room into which she had bought him was a study in peach and dove grey, a beautifully proportioned room, big yet cosy and relaxed. Keith, faced with solving such an enormous crime would normally have been tense, antennae out, on the twitch. Instead, he felt almost relaxed. He knew why, of course. From the moment he had shaken hands with Bettine Irving, he had already decided that she had no part to play in whatever had happened to her husband, her son or the poor girl lying dead in her hall.

They had not met before. Sir Hugo's disappearance had been dealt with by the local force and the coastguards and by the time it was considered likely that Sir Hugo was dead and Keith became involved, Lady Irving was already back in London and the matter was dealt with by the Met. Coffee was served by an enormous, smiling Caribbean lady who fussed over Keith making him feel even more comfortable and pampered – razor-sharp he was not. Before he could begin interviewing Lady Irving, she began questioning him – wide grey eyes above a distinguished aquiline nose. 'Who is the poor girl, Chief Inspector, do you know yet?'

Keith shook his head. 'She was carrying no identity, or rather there was certainly no identity on the body when we found her. We are obviously checking for fingerprints and taking DNA samples. I believe the local boys already have yours, Lady Irving.' She nodded. 'Obviously what we are trying to do is to eliminate the family and see who else has been to the house.'

'Apart, I suppose, from the murderer, there shouldn't be traces of anyone else,' said Lady Irving. 'You've presumably included Jenny our cleaner?' Keith nodded. 'The thing about our home in St Ives, is that we went there to get away from all this,' she indicated the room. 'My husband leads, led, a very busy life both in business and socially and the demands on him and to a lesser extent – a much lesser of course – on me meant that when we were in Cornwall the last thing we wanted to do was to socialise.'

'I understand,' said Keith, and he did.

'Hugo used to surf and I pottered about in the garden, went to the Tate and sat and read the papers in the sun, that sort of thing.' Her voice was wistful and Keith realised that she probably could not imagine ever being able to live that sort of life again – to be that relaxed, be that content.

'I have to ask you two questions,' said Keith, 'which will be painful, but I need you to think very carefully and answer them to the very best of your ability.' Lady Irving squared her shoulders and met his eye.

'Go on,' she said.

'Do you believe your husband is dead?' She lowered her head for a moment and stared at her hands, clasped in her lap.

'I didn't,' she said, looking up at Keith after a moment, 'not to start with. I suppose it was too great a shock to handle and then there was the fact that he was such a good swimmer, such an experienced surfer …' her voice trailed away, '… but I do now.'

'And when did you change your mind?'

'Oh, I suppose about a week after it happened. Initially I expected him to walk through the door any moment and then the surfboard was found but no body …' her voice trailed away.

'But as he was such a good swimmer, didn't you find his death hard to accept?'

'I did, I still do,' said Lady Irving. 'I've been through it a million times, as you can imagine. I can only assume that he must have had a heart attack, or a stroke. Something must have caused him to …' her voice broke slightly, 'lose consciousness and he drowned.'

'And Miles?' Keith asked, gently. The reaction to her son was very different. Instead of the calm, sadness she was immediately agitated.

'I take it there has been no news?' She asked, tears starting in her eyes.

Keith shook his head. 'Nothing at all, and you, I assume, you haven't heard from him?'

She shook her head, the tears began to spill down her cheeks, she bit her lip and twisted her hands in her lap. 'I just don't understand it, I just can't think what can have happened to him. You don't think he had anything to do with the girl's death, do you? He wouldn't, I know he couldn't hurt anyone, he is such a gentle young man.'

Keith sidestepped the question. 'I've talked to one or two people,' he said, 'and I get the impression that your son was rather overawed by your husband.'

She was dabbing her eyes with her handkerchief. 'I'm sorry,' she said, 'It is just such a dreadful time, could you give me a moment.'

'Of course,' said Keith. 'I understand completely.'

They sat in silence for a few moments. Then Bettine rallied. 'Yes, yes he was rather overawed by Hugo, it's true. Miles is quite timid, artistic. His real talent is in music. He should be going to the Royal College, I'm sure he would get in but my husband insisted he went to Bristol University instead.'

'What is he going to study there?' Keith asked.

'Business Studies,' said Lady Irving, hardly able to contain her contempt. 'It's the last thing he should be doing. Perhaps that's the only good thing to come out of all this – perhaps he will be free to do as he wishes.'

'As you know,' said Keith, after a pause, 'he was due to meet me in St Ives.'

'But he never came, did he, Chief Inspector? I last saw him at breakfast on the day he was due to catch the sleeper. I went out for lunch with a friend and did not see him again.' She put her hand to her mouth, trying not to cry.

Keith pressed on. 'I've checked with your cleaner, Jenny. She went up to the house shortly after ten the previous night when Miles was supposed to have arrived. She was surprised to find he wasn't there. By the time I arrived the following afternoon, at three, there was just the body. There was no sign of forced entry, the front and the back doors were both locked. None of the other rooms appear to have been disturbed or used in any way. She, the young girl,' he hesitated, 'clearly died in the hall.'

'She was stabbed, I understand?' Lady Irving said, faintly. Keith nodded. 'It's horrible, too horrible,' she said.

'Did your son, does your son,' he corrected himself hurriedly, 'have a girlfriend?'

'No,' said Lady Irving, 'not at the moment. As I say, he is very shy and rather young for his age. He has friends from school of course but there hasn't really been a serious girlfriend yet.'

'Are you sure?' said Keith. 'He is eighteen, isn't he?'

'I'm quite sure.'

There was a lengthy silence. 'So where do you think your son is now, Lady Irving?'

There was a catch in her voice. 'I don't know, Chief Inspector. I have absolutely no idea, but I do know without a shadow of a doubt that whoever killed that poor young girl, it wasn't Miles.'

Now, leaning back on his chair, staring sightlessly out of the window, he found it hard, no impossible, not to believe her. Her reactions had been so true, so as they should be, they smacked of integrity. She was clearly devastated by her husband's disappearance but after four months she had her emotions under control. Not so with regard to her son. She was in pieces, and who wouldn't be in the circumstances? What had caused father and son to disappear? Was their disappearance linked in some way and what in God's name was the dead girl doing there? Forensics had come up with very little so far, other than the fact that the young woman had been in her early twenties and, she was almost certainly a prostitute.

'She's got every sort of clap known to man or beast,' the pathologist had told Keith none too delicately. Pathology agreed with Keith that she was probably not English, eastern European most likely, possibly Polish. After cleaning her up they had managed to create a reasonable image of her and even now her picture was being shown around well-known red light districts in both London and Cornwall in the hope that someone might recognise her. London and Cornwall were a shot in the dark – the search assumed some connection with the Irvings. Poor girl, she had to be someone's daughter, probably someone's sister, maybe even someone's mother. As always his mind turned towards Carly, his daughter – at least she was loved and cherished. The irony was not lost on him. Here was a poor girl who had ended up with the dregs of a life yet, despite everything, was still probably healthier than his own daughter who had never known a day's deprivation.

Sometimes of late he was starting to feel too old, too disillusioned to enjoy his job any more. He let out a sigh and took a swig from a near-cold cup of coffee, which helped him in no way at all. All his life in the police force he had seen his role as trying to save humanity from itself, doing what he could to keep society safe; to help, not just the good guys, but the bad guys too sometimes; trying to find a balance, a way for people to live together in harmony. Lately though, he felt he was in a losing battle and he was lucky enough to be based in Cornwall. He could not even imagine what it must be like for his colleagues up-country. It was the young who upset him most –

throwing their lives away in a blur of drugs, drink and excess of every kind. This poor girl was not like that, though. She was a victim, he knew that instinctively and as the word 'instinctively' came into his mind, he could not help but think of Felicity Paradise. She had an instinct for things. What would she make of Miles's disappearance which, of course, she must know about from the media? Perhaps the best thing to do was simply to ask her.

6

She was enormously flattered. Throughout her relationship with Keith Penrose, Felicity had always been asking him for the favours, trying to prove to him her suspicions and her belief when something was wrong. One way and another, she had invested a lot of time trying to persuade him to take her seriously and now, at last, it appeared that he was; he needed her – it was quite extraordinary.

Over the three years that they had known one another he had teased her gently and sometimes not so gently about what he called her 'supposed second sight'. He didn't deny its existence but nor was he a signed up member. Apart from her children, who simply took her moments of second sight in their stride, accepting it as much a part of her as the mole on her neck, there were only three other people in the world who had ever truly believed in her gift – her mother, her husband and her best friend from school days, Gilly. Her mother, long dead now, did not have the gift herself but her mother, Felicity's grandmother, had and her mother before that. For

Charlie and Gilly it was simply a question of having know Felicity for so long, after a while, they came to recognise that her moments of second sight were no affectation, but a reality, which could and should be taken seriously.

As she toiled up the hill beside Keith Penrose on their way to the Irvings' house, she was full of apprehension. The one thing she definitely could not claim to be was a clairvoyant. Felicity could not call upon her ability to see things – just sometimes she did, but never to order. On occasion she was shocked by the suddenness and clarity of what she saw, other times there was just a suspicion, a feeling, a sense, a shadow. They opened the wrought-iron gate and climbed the steps up onto the terrace.

'It's a beautiful view from here,' said Keith conversationally in an attempt to ease the tension, but Felicity's mind was elsewhere. She felt sick with nerves, her own or someone else's, she was not sure. Keith sensed that all was not well. 'Look, if this is too much for you just say so. I don't want to put you through this if you're going to be distressed by it. I'm asking a lot, I know that.'

Felicity tried to smile. 'It's OK, honestly, I want to help, I really do.'

'Come on then,' he said, smiling back, 'I'm going to take you around the back of the house so that we come into the hall as Jack and I did. That way I can explain exactly what we saw in context.'

They walked around to the rear of the house and ducked under the police tape. Keith unlocked the back door and ushered her into the kitchen. She stood in the centre of the room and was suddenly overwhelmed by a sense of dread. Again she was unsure whether it was her own or someone else's.

'Ready?' Keith asked. 'I'll go first.' He opened the kitchen door and turned right into the hall. It was little more than a passage leading to the front door. The sun was streaming through the stained glass panel that was the centrepiece of the front door. They had done their best to clean up. There were still brown stains on the carpet and the walls on either side were very discoloured. Felicity shuddered. Keith stood close by her.

'She was lying with her head nearest the front door,' he said, 'on her side, curled up almost in the foetal position. Her arms were over her head obviously trying to protect herself. She had nine stab wounds and as you can see from what remains of the stains, there was blood everywhere. It was a very violent attack, anger was involved, I sense.'

'Could you leave me alone for a moment?' Felicity asked, in a very strained voice.

Keith put a hand on her arm. 'Are you sure?' She nodded, already distracted, and taking the hint he withdrew to the kitchen.

She knew she was not going to see what had happened but she felt a real sense of terror now, which she was certain, was not her own. She tried to harness it, accept it, make it a part of herself and see what happened next. In her mind she walked to the front door. Was it in response to a knock or a ring on the bell? It was a ring on the bell. As she opened the door sun streamed in, it was very hot. The figure standing before her was tall and thickset, a brute of a man with a swarthy complexion and a small, straggly beard. At the sight of him, the terror intensified, overtook her and she began to scream. Keith was beside her in a second. She was shaking from head to foot, there were tears in her eyes and she was white as a sheet.

He put his arm around her. 'I'm sorry, I'm so sorry. I shouldn't have done this to you.'

'It's alright,' she broke free of his arm, 'but please, please could we get out of here?'

'Yes, of course,' he started to usher her towards the front door.

'No, no,' she almost shouted, 'not the front door, please. Could we go round the back again, now?'

He led her back through the kitchen. As soon as she was out she bolted round to the front of the house and was down the steps and out of the gate in the time it took Keith to lock up behind him.

'Where shall we go?' he asked.

'Anywhere but here.'

The town was full to bursting. 'I think perhaps I should take you home,' he said.

'I think perhaps you should,' she replied.

Once in her own kitchen the trembling eased a little. She shakily put on the kettle, clumsily made tea and they sat down beside one another at the kitchen table.

'I'm sorry,' Keith said again.

'No, it's alright. Let me tell you what happened while it is still fresh in my mind.'

'Go on,' said Keith. He produced a notebook from his pocket.

'I think I became the victim. I felt terrified as soon as I was in the hall, it's why I asked you to go, I needed to hang on to the emotion and not be sidetracked. In my head I went to answer the front door, somebody had rung the bell. I opened the door and there was a man standing there.'

'Did you see what he looked like?' Keith asked.

'Yes, I did,' said Felicity. As she spoke she felt the fear again. 'He was a tall man, well built, not dark skinned, but sallow, with a beard.'

'A big beard?' Keith asked.

'No, a sort of straggly and unkempt affair.'

'Age?'

'I'm not sure,' said Felicity. 'Middle years somewhere, he wasn't young and he wasn't old.'

'What happened then?'

'I was terrified and I screamed – sorry, it all sounds rather pathetic.'

'No, no, not at all. If one is to believe in your gift, then you have just given me a description of the killer. Is there anything else you can add?'

'Yes, it was daylight and the sun was streaming straight in the front door.'

Keith gave a sigh of satisfaction and smiled at her. 'Well done, that fits perfectly. The time of death is estimated to be somewhere between twelve and one o'clock on the afternoon that Jack and I visited the house. We only missed it by an hour or so.'

Felicity stared at him, her eyes wide with horror.

'It happened while you and I were having lunch.' Keith nodded. 'How awful, if I hadn't rung up and asked you out for lunch then …'

'No,' said Keith, vehemently 'no, don't go down that road. I had already made my appointment with Miles for three o'clock. That's what was agreed long before you telephoned me; our lunch made no difference at all.'

'Honestly?' she asked.

'Honestly, I promise. Tell me, this feeling you had, do you think you knew the killer?'

Felicity considered the question. 'I think I must have done, because otherwise why would I have been so frightened at the sight of him?'

'But you let him in.'

'I don't think I was expecting it to be him. I was shocked and frightened at the sight of him, but he wasn't who I was expecting. The image stopped before the attack, but I'm sure I was really surprised to see him, I was shocked as well as terrified.'

'Then it sounds like you definitely knew him.'

'Yes,' said Felicity. 'Yes, I think so. I suspect he must have killed her immediately she opened the door. I think he must have pushed her into the hall, shut the door and then killed her.'

'That fits in with the fact that there was clearly no disturbance in the rest of the house, and it also explains why there was no sign of a break in.'

'I keep thinking,' said Felicity, after a pause, 'that terror I felt, I was able to run away from it, escape – that poor girl, there was no such escape for her.'

'You're a nice person,' Keith said gently.

'Not really, but I have thought of something which is cheering. The man I told you about, he doesn't sound much like Miles Irving?'

'No,' said Inspector Penrose, with a smile. 'He certainly doesn't. Do you think if we got an artist involved you could try and create an image of this man? Though God knows what I'm letting myself in for, I'll be the laughing stock at the station.'

'Really,' said Felicity, 'why?'

'We do sometimes seek help from clairvoyants and the like but on the whole all that sort of stuff is pretty much frowned upon and considered to be a lot of mumbo jumbo. I think we should take what you have seen seriously, but there will be a lot of scepticism. I'll just have to broaden my shoulders, and pull rank.'

'Now you're a Chief Inspector,' said Felicity with a smile, 'you're probably exempt from the teasing.'

'I very much doubt it,' said Keith, 'but I do have

faith in you, Mrs Paradise, and I will have to hope that sustains me.'

'I find that deeply touching, Chief Inspector.' And she did.

Felicity spent the afternoon in Truro with an artist doing her best to recreate the face of the man she had seen. It was made more difficult, she realised, because the sun was shining directly from behind him and so his face had been partially in shadow. When she had finished she was called to Keith's office.

'So is this a good likeness?' He waved the drawing at her.

She studied it in silence for a moment. 'I couldn't just fiddle with it for a second, could I?'

'In what way?' he asked.

'Maybe if you took a photocopy and let me play with that then I won't mess up the original.'

'Of course,' he said, 'I was forgetting you are an artist. Hang on a moment.'

He returned with two copies and handed one to Felicity.

'Do you have a pencil or a black felt tip and something I can lean on? She asked. 'I can see there's no space on your desk – some things never change.'

He ignored her and patted piles of paper on his desk, until finally he produced a black biro. 'Will that do?'

'That'll be fine.'

'And a Yellow Pages to lean on?'

She nodded and thanked him. 'You would have thought,' she said, as she studied the face in front of her, 'that now you're a Chief Inspector, you'd feel you ought to set an example by tidying up this place. It's worse than ever, it's an absolute tip.'

'It's how I work,' he said, firmly.

'Apparently so,' she said with a smile. 'The nose isn't quite right, it was a little longer, sharper.' She doodled away with it until she had it to her satisfaction. 'The eyebrows were thicker, heavier and virtually joined at the middle.' She studied the effect, 'and his eyes were more sunken in, less prominent,' she added a few strokes under each eye and suddenly, out of nowhere, the fear was back. 'Got it!' she said, tremulously.

'Really, are you sure?'

She nodded and handed the sheet to him. 'Yes, he's frightening me now.'

'I'm not surprised he's a terrible-looking chap, a positive stereotype of evil. So now you've done the mug shot, can you give us a clue as to what he was wearing?'

'I'm sorry,' said Felicity, 'I have absolutely no idea. All I can say is that his clothing was dark, but apart from the fact that he was a chunky, burly man of medium height, I can tell you nothing.'

'This really is a great help.' He was about to stand up to see her out when his mobile rang. 'Would you excuse me?' He was listening intently doodling on the pad in front of him as he did so. Suddenly the doodling stopped. 'What!' he shouted into the telephone, 'are you absolutely sure, and what about the parents?' He listened again. 'Good God what on earth have we got here? Well, thanks very much, Jim, I'll be back to you.' Keith replaced the receiver and stared at Felicity. 'I suppose I shouldn't be telling you this but I just don't know what the hell to make of it.'

'What?' Felicity asked, seeing his shock, his incredulity.

'We took DNA samples of everyone – the girl, Lady Irving, hair from Miles's brush, the cleaner and we already had Sir Hugo's. It appears that the dead girl and Miles are closely related, almost certainly siblings.'

'Good grief,' said Felicity, 'are they sure?'

'Absolutely, the lab checked it two or three times, they couldn't believe it either.'

'And the parents, Miles's parents.'

'Sir Hugo and Lady Irving are not related to anyone.'

'What, not even to Miles?'

'Nope.'

'What, neither of them?'

'No, I thought Lady Irving looked nervous when I mentioned the DNA. She must have been worried this would come out.'

'But what exactly has come out?' Felicity asked, frowning.

'I'm not sure,' said Keith. 'It's not unusual to find

that the father is not the father, but, in this case, the fact that neither of the parents are related to their son is odd and even odder that he is related to the dead girl on their hall carpet. God knows what it means, God knows what we're going to unravel.'

'Miles must have been adopted,' Felicity said, after a moment.

'It's the first I've heard of it,' said Keith.

'Why should you?' said Felicity. 'I mean, it's nobody's business but theirs. They had a child before Miles, if you remember. Maybe after the tragedy of her death, they found they couldn't have any more children.'

'So you're saying, because they couldn't have another child they adopted instead?'

'They were certainly quite old to have Miles naturally,' said Felicity. 'At least, I don't know about Lady Irving but Sir Hugo was certainly quite old to have an eighteen year old son.'

'She's much the same age as he is – was, whatever,' Keith said. 'She is very well preserved, but certainly not in her first youth.'

They sat in silence, both lost in thought.

'So what next?' Felicity asked.

Keith Penrose was suddenly galvanised into action. He stood up and made for the door, Felicity's drawing in hand. 'This mug shot, considering the circumstances, I daren't put it out on general circulation, but I will make sure my team have it, and take seriously the notion that this is the man we are seeking in connection with that poor girl's murder. Then it looks like I'm getting that damned sleeper back up to London. Lady Irving has some explaining to do.'

7

Anya Cascescu sat alone on the edge of the bed. She was exhausted, terrified. Never had she felt so alone. Marianna had been like a big sister to her and now she was dead. The man, Steve, had made Anya and the other two girls move flats during the night. One of the other girls had explained it to her – Steve was frightened that the men who visited them might recognise Marianna from the television pictures and might tell the police where she had worked.

As soon as she heard that Marianna was dead, Anya knew that Steve had killed her. Stabbed nine times, one of the girls had told her. The other girls were stupid, they said Steve was not a murderer but she knew they were wrong, she knew what he could do.

Yet again she walked over to the tiny window of the room where she was being held prisoner. She was five floors up and there was no means of escape. Steve hadn't bothered to lock the window because he didn't have to, but he had locked the door. He let her out now and again for the bathroom. He gave her water and a little food, otherwise she just sat there with her thoughts. She had to get away, she had to go to the police and tell them what Steve had done, she had to do it for Marianna's sake, for her own sake, for all the girls in her situation.

The trouble was she didn't speak English, except for the stupid words she had been taught to say to keep the men happy. How would she find a police station? How would she get there and what would happen if Steve caught her? He would kill her too. She started to cry and that made her angry. At sixteen she was too old to cry. She needed to be strong, crying was weak. She was in terrible trouble, worse trouble than she had ever been in her short miserable life but she wasn't crying for her mother – she had never had one of those.

Keith Penrose sensed he was not so welcome this time, there was something in Lady Irving's face which was different. She was shuttered off, polite but cool.

'I take it you have no news of my son, Chief Inspector?' she asked.

'Nothing yet, Lady Irving, and you?'

She shook her head. 'I of course would have let you know straight away if I had heard from him.'

'I do have some news with regard to our investigation into the murder at your holiday home,' Keith began, without preamble.

'Oh good,' said Lady Irving, coolly. 'Have you

caught the person responsible?'

'No, not yet,' said Keith.

'Have ...' she hesitated, 'have you a suspect?'

'We have an idea what the suspect looks like.'

'Then ...' she hesitated again, 'you don't suspect Miles?'

Keith sighed. 'We'd very much like to interview Miles. He was supposed to be in the house at the time of the murder, but no, he is not our prime suspect at the moment.'

During their conversation Lady Irving had been standing by the fireplace. Now, clearly relieved at his words, she sat down in a chair. 'So, what can I do for you Chief Inspector?' she asked, slightly warmer now.

'I was wondering when you were going to tell me that Miles is not your son?'

'He is my son!' she said immediately angry and defensive.

'By birth I meant.'

She went white as a sheet. 'How do you know?'

'DNA,' said Keith. 'He is clearly not the product of either you or your husband. How can that be?'

'He is adopted,' said Lady Irving.

'It might have been helpful if we had known that,' said Keith.

'Why?' she flashed. 'I don't see it is relevant to anything nor any business of yours.'

'When did you adopt him and in what circumstances?'

'From Romania, he was adopted from Romania.'

'When would that have been?'

'In 1990.'

'So,' said Keith, 'he would have been two?' Lady Irving nodded. 'You are a high profile family, I'm surprised nothing has been made of it by the press.'

'No one knew,' said Lady Irving. 'In that period my husband was developing his business interests in Australia, and we moved there with him for a couple of years. By the time we came back to England, Miles was four and everyone assumed he was our son by birth.'

'And you didn't disillusion them?'

'There was no need. As I said it is nobody's business but ours.' Lady Irving was icy.

'It is Miles's business so I presume he knows?' Briefly, her eyes slid away from Keith's.

'Oh, my God,' said Keith, 'he doesn't know either, does he?'

'We didn't think it was a good thing to tell him. He seemed to have blocked out the first two years of his life, so we felt it best to leave it at that. What possible use could it be for him to know his background when it was so ... so awful.'

'I would have thought he had the right to know,' said Keith, trying none too successfully to suppress his anger. He was shocked to the core. He couldn't believe a woman as intelligent as this could make such a crass error. He frowned. 'What about his passport and birth certificate, surely that would have alerted him to his adoptive status.'

'They have a funny system in Romania, or at least they did at the time,' said Lady Irving. 'Firstly, before you could bring a child out of Romania they had to be adopted there and then you had to re-adopt them in your own country. So in order to let the children out of the country, they had to have a Romanian passport and the passport place of birth was given as the parents' town of residence, so on Miles's Romanian passport it said his place of birth was London. When he eventually received his UK passport, I presume they simply copied the details and in doing so made a mistake. The mistake was what prompted us to conceal the adoption. He was a very vulnerable little boy and we decided it was better to put his past behind him once and for all. I don't regret the decision, Chief Inspector, and I think at the time it was reasonable to assume that we were not going to be in the centre of a murder investigation which might reveal Miles's origins.'

The atmosphere in the room was crackling with suppressed anger. What Keith had to tell Lady Irving, he knew, was likely to come as a terrible shock and he had to fight the very strong desire to use it as a weapon. He played for time. 'What about Miles's birth family, have you ever kept in touch with them?'

'What birth family?' Lady Irving, scoffed. 'Miles came from a Romanian orphanage, I don't know whether you remember the press at the time, Chief Inspector, but thousands of Romanian children were simply abandoned in appalling institutions, in truly terrible circumstances. We don't consider we did Miles a disservice by rescuing him from that.'

'I would agree with you there, Lady Irving,' said Keith, quietly, 'I just wondered whether you had kept in touch with his family.'

'Some adoptive parents did trace relatives, but as far as we were concerned, they gave up their rights to him when he was abandoned in the orphanage.'

'But there must have been parents on his birth certificate.'

'Yes, there were as I recall, but they had no objection to him being adopted and no wish to have anything to do with him in the future.'

'And siblings?' Keith asked.

'I have no idea whether the family gave all their children away or kept some. It's an extraordinary part of the world, the rules that apply to a normal civilised society simply don't work over there.

'I thought the problem was that many of the parents couldn't afford to keep their children,' said Keith, evenly. 'It's very hard in my view to judge people when their circumstances are so remote from one's own.'

If Lady Irving recognised this as a rebuke, she said nothing. The silence stretched out between them.

Keith took a deep breath. 'Then I think, Lady Irving, it is going to come as a considerable shock to you to learn that the girl found dead in the hallway of your holiday home was, in fact, a close relation to

Miles, almost certainly his sister.' He leaned forward, prepared to move swiftly if Lady Irving appeared to be likely to faint. For a moment she swayed and he stood up hurriedly, moving towards her. She put out a hand to fend him off.

'I'm perfectly alright, Chief Inspector.'

He stood uncertainly halfway between her chair and his. For something to do and to give her a moment he turned his back on her and walked over to the window. The street scene outside seemed very tranquil compared with the turmoil of feelings swirling round in this elegant drawing room.

'I presume you are absolutely certain of your facts, Chief Inspector,' Lady Irving said, after a moment.

He turned to face her, she was very pale, but still seemed relatively composed.

'Absolutely,' he said, 'you can be certain I wouldn't have passed this information on to you unless I was completely certain of my facts.'

'No, no, of course not.'

'Can you explain it?' he asked.

She shook her head slowly. 'I can only assume that one of his siblings must have had access to his Romanian adoption papers and found out where he was and decided to make contact. Bearing in mind the family he's adopted into, she was probably after money.'

Again, Keith felt a surge of anger, which he had to fight to control.

'You don't know it was anything to do with money, Lady Irving,' he said, evenly, 'it's not unreasonable to suppose that a sister would want to track down a long lost brother out of love, or out of hope of love.' Again the silence was protracted. 'So you are saying that neither you, nor your husband, had any knowledge of there being a sister.'

'No,' said Lady Irving.

'And because Miles is unaware of his adoptive status he, of course, does not believe he has a sister.'

'He does believe he has a sister,' Lady Irving said.

Keith frowned.

'He believes he has a sister who died at four from meningitis before he was born. That's his real sister.'

'Over that, and many other views you have expressed during this interview,' said Keith, 'I'm afraid I must beg to differ.'

The Romanian Embassy proved extremely helpful and within twenty-four hours of his interview with Lady Irving, Keith had established that Marianna and Nicholae Ivanovitch had been placed in the notorious Orphanage Number 1 in Bucharest shortly after Nicholae's birth. There they had remained sharing a cot, according to a nurse who had been interviewed by the solicitor in charge of the adoption, until Nicholae was taken from the orphanage to become Miles Irving. Marianna had stayed at the orphanage until she was sixteen, when she ran away, and had not been heard of since, until, that is, her dead body turned up in St Ives. At the time of her death she was twenty-one years and seven months, three and a half years older than her brother.

Armed with the tragedy of this story, Keith found on his return from London, he could not stay in his office – he needed to talk it through with somebody with an understanding of families, somebody who cared passionately about children, someone who could help him through the minefield of emotions that seemed to be overwhelming him. He climbed into his car and took the A30 to St Ives.

8

Felicity and Orlando were planning a quiet evening in front of the television. Felicity had spent all day painting and was weary, her eyes hurt, her hand shook, it was time to stop. The cat fed, she was dithering about whether to have a glass of white wine, there was half a bottle open in the fridge, or to open a bottle of red which she, at this moment, preferred. There was a ring on the front door bell. Annie, Felicity imagined, with her latest titbit of gossip. She ran down the stairs and opened the door. There, standing in the light drizzle, was the rather forlorn figure of Chief Inspector Keith Penrose.

'Goodness,' said Felicity, 'you look bedraggled.'

'I'm feeling bedraggled. Are you busy or could you spare me a few moments?'

She smiled. 'Actually, you've just solved a problem for me.'

'Really?' he said coming in through the door and removing a very damp jacket, 'I'm naturally pleased to be able to solve your problem, but I was rather hoping you might solve mine.'

Up in the kitchen Felicity set two glasses on the table.

'All you have to do to solve my problem is to agree to have a glass of red wine, then I have an excuse to open a bottle.'

'Problem solved,' said Keith, with a smile.

Glasses in hand they went through into Felicity's cosy little sitting room. A wood fire spluttered in the grate and they sat down either side of it in companionable silence for a moment.

'What a charming room,' said Keith.

'It's lovely in the winter,' Felicity said, 'but on a chilly evening like this, even in summer, I can't resist lighting the fire.'

Keith smiled. 'You're really settled here now, aren't you?'

'Yes,' Felicity acknowledged, with a faint smile.

'So, even with your family up-country, you wouldn't go back?'

She shook her head. 'No, my life is here now.'

'I'm glad,' he hesitated. 'I don't know what we'd all do without you,' he said a little gruffly, staring fixedly at the fire, clearly embarrassed.

'You'd all be just fine, I'm sure,' said Felicity, anxious to lighten the mood. 'Now what can I do for you?'

Keith leant back in his chair. 'The pieces are falling in place, up to a point. I just know I'm missing something, something major. Actually, that's not right either, I haven't a clue what's going on, and that's the truth.'

'Tell me,' said Felicity, gently.

'You were right. Miles Irving was adopted from a Romanian orphanage when he was twenty months old.'

Felicity frowned. 'How come that's never been an issue in the press?'

'The Irvings went to great lengths to conceal the fact that he was adopted and it was made easy for them because they were living in Australia at the time while Sir Hugo was building his empire. When they returned to the UK their friends just assumed that the boy had been born out there.'

'Well, there's nothing particularly wrong about that is there? If that's how they felt. It is, after all, a private matter and they probably wanted to shield Miles from the press, being such a high profile family,' Felicity said.

'I think it becomes wrong,' Keith said, slowly, 'if they not only misled their friends but they also misled Miles.'

'You mean Miles doesn't know he was adopted?'

Keith shook his head.

'That is awful,' Felicity agreed, 'they shouldn't have kept it from him. In any event, he was bound to find out one day, in fact, he must have known, deep down, all through his life I would have thought.'

'Certainly it explains why he is nothing like Sir Hugo.' said Keith, 'He is very musical, apparently, and shy. You could hardly call Sir Hugo shy.'

Felicity smiled and nodded her head in agreement.

'I contacted the Romanian Embassy and eventually through them a Romanian lawyer in Bucharest, who spoke very good English. Miles was born Nicholae Ivanovitch and he had a sister, Marianna, who was three and a half years older than him. The children appear to have been put into an orphanage when Miles was born.'

'Together?' Felicity asked.

Keith nodded.

'Then why in God's name didn't the Irvings adopt both children?'

Keith shook his head. 'I haven't raised that with Lady Irving, because she maintains she didn't know there was a sister. I imagine to have adopted a little girl would seem like trying to replace the child who died. Maybe in fairness that's why they didn't or maybe they wanted a child without baggage and they reckoned Miles was young enough to put his past behind him, whereas Marianna might not have been able to do so.'

'So,' said Felicity, 'the children were separated when the Irvings took Miles and they never met again, or did they?'

'That's what keeps going round and round in my mind,' said Keith, 'and that's why I'm here really. I cannot believe that Miles killed his sister, I cannot believe, although I've never met him, that Miles could kill anyone. Yet back at the station your bearded friend is considered to be something of a joke and everyone else feels it is a foregone conclusion that Miles is responsible for his sister's death – couldn't handle the shock of his past, that sort of thing.'

Felicity was silent for a few moments, frowning in concentration. 'If they did meet,' she said at last, 'Miles would have had a double shock – firstly that he was adopted and that his parents had chosen to keep the knowledge from him, and secondly that he had a sister and here she was – from what you have told me of Miles, he is very sensitive, vulnerable, thin skinned, as my mother used to say. In my view there is no way such a person would react to that news by dashing into the kitchen, grabbing a knife and stabbing his sister. He'd be deeply traumatised, certainly, but surely if he did anything dramatic, he would simply run away from it all.'

Keith's head jerked up and he stared at Felicity. 'So you're saying that confronted with the news of his adoption and with the evidence of his sister before him, he'd have simply run out on her?'

'It would have been a lot to cope with all at once. It is a possible reaction, I would have thought.'

'So,' said Keith, 'Marianna arrives at the Irvings' family home – how on earth did she find them incidentally?'

'That's simple enough,' said Felicity, 'with all the publicity there has been surrounding Sir Hugo's disappearance recently and all of it based in St Ives, she'd have probably imagined that's where they lived.'

'So,' said Keith, 'she turns up at the Irvings' family home and Miles is already there. He was supposed to be, after all.'

'Maybe when the housekeeper, Jenny, called round the night before, Miles was already in town. From what you've told me, he doesn't sound like the sort to be out on the razzle all night, but he could have met a friend for a drink when he got off the train.'

'That sounds logical,' said Keith, 'but it doesn't fit.'

'Why not, he wouldn't have had to come home very late to miss Jenny.'

'He didn't come down the night before,' said Keith, 'because none of the bedrooms were disturbed. He must have come down early the following day, the day of the murder – if he came down at all that is. There is absolutely no evidence that he was ever in St Ives. We've checked the trains, no one remembers him.'

'OK, but supposing he did come down the following day and he was in the house when Marianna arrived,' said Felicity, on her feet now, pacing around. 'She told him who she was, it would have all been very emotional and maybe he just couldn't cope with it, maybe he ran out on her.'

'And she waited at the house for him to return?' Keith said.

'And while Miles was ranting on the beach or whatever, the killer struck,' Felicity finished for him. 'But then who was the killer?'

'Poor Marianna was a prostitute, almost certainly,' said Keith, 'so I presume the killer might have been her pimp. There are so many rackets going on at the moment, particularly where Eastern European girls are concerned. There are hundreds of appalling cases of young girls being bought into the country under the pretence of domestic work, when, in reality, they become sex slaves. Marianna would have been a natural victim, presumably. Prostitution may well have been her way of life before she left Romania. After the orphanage she would have had no one to support her. At some stage, presumably she made her own enquiries as to what happened to her brother. Having learnt he was adopted by a couple from the UK she would have been particularly anxious to come here to try and find him. It made her easy prey. She was such a pretty girl, too. A tragedy, the whole thing's a tragedy.' Sitting slumped in the chair, Keith suddenly seemed very much his age, and utterly defeated. Felicity had never seen him like this before and it shocked her.

'I've never seen you this low,' she said, 'what's caused it?'

'Oh, I don't know,' he said, 'it's just such a mess, young lives destroyed.'

'It's children, isn't it?' Felicity said, with a sudden flash of insight. 'You can't bear awful things happening to children. I noticed that when little George Gresham went missing, you were in a real state.'

Keith met her eye. 'No, I suppose you're right. Children are my Achilles heel, I always dread it when I become involved with a case where a child has been abused or damaged in some way.' He smiled at her, drained his glass and stood up. 'I don't know, maybe I'm getting soft in my old age. It's just that man's inhumanity to man seems to be getting to me a bit. I long ago abandoned aspirations to change the world, to make it a better place, but the status quo would be nice, yet at the moment we seem to be on some self-destruct course, as far as I can see.'

'Dear, dear,' said Felicity, she smiled gently at him, 'you are in a bad way.' She rested her hand lightly on his arm.

'I'm sorry,' he said, 'I just can't get the image out of my mind of these two little children abandoned at the orphanage and then separated. Then against all the odds they meet again but before they could even get to know one another, the girl ends up dead.'

'I know what you mean,' said Felicity, 'of course I do, and I also believe that your instincts are right. I cannot believe Miles Irving killed his sister and, and …' she hesitated, 'I know you're not wholly convinced by my strange little episodes of second sight, or whatever you call them, but I am absolutely certain that Marianna was scared witless by the man I described to you and sadly it seems logical that someone who could terrify her so much is likely to be the person who killed her.'

9

If you are alone and lost, cold and soaked through, hungry and frightened, a stranger in a strange land, then what you need is a guardian angel.

A large curly-haired dog pressing a sandy nose against your cheek was not an obvious candidate and yet, Anya felt comforted. She fondled his ears and he wagged his tail in response and gave her a rather fishy lick on the cheek. Then, as quickly as he had come, he turned and bounded off into the night.

Left alone in the dark Anya began to shake with cold. What on earth had possessed her to come here, it made no sense, what was she trying to achieve? Her friend, the girl who had been like a big sister to her, a mother almost, was dead. Coming to the place where she had died – she had to be crazy, there was no point – it was stupid, stupid. At the time it had seemed logical. Steve, high on drink or drugs had left her door unlocked. Alone in a London Street, she could only think of the journey Marianna had rehearsed again and again – the train from Paddington, how to hide in the toilets when the ticket inspector comes by, how to get out at St Erth, change onto a little train to St Ives. She had followed Marianna's journey, she was amazed that she had been able to do it. It had taken hours, she had no idea St Ives was so far away from London but here she was in the place where Marianna had died – and now what?

She had arrived late afternoon and had spent the few pence she had on a cup of coffee. Instinctively she'd liked the place, it was a pretty town and the people so relaxed and friendly compared with London. She had made her way to the harbour, she had walked down the slipway and along the beach until she had found a little place against the harbour wall which was protected from the wind but in the sun. She had settled there and gone to sleep, exhausted from her journey and her terror. When she had woken the sun had gone and then out of nowhere there was a short, sharp shower of rain which left her wet through. She huddled against the harbour wall and as darkness fell, with the shouts of holiday makers partying above her, she was paralysed by her own disorientation and terror.

Felicity met Henry and Archie on the wharf. They were walking briskly, Henry explained, having just completed a circuit of the Island.

'Extraordinary,' said Henry, 'the town's heaving with holidaymakers but they never go up onto the Island at night or walk round by Breakwater. It's like living in two towns. Where are you bound?'

'I'm doing your walk in reverse,' said Felicity, 'I've been working all day and I just needed a breath of fresh air before bedtime.'

'You should have a dog,' said Henry, 'a companion makes a walk so much more worthwhile.'

'I absolutely agree,' said Felicity, 'but I have an aged cat who would not tolerate a puppy at this stage in his life.'

'Talking of companions,' Henry looked around him, 'where has Archie gone?' On cue Archie appeared beside them, he was agitated, barking, backing away. 'Oh, now what?' Henry said. 'I'd better go and investigate, it's probably a piece of dead fish he's got to show me but after Sir Hugo Irving's discarded beachwear I'm honour bound to take Archie's instructions seriously.'

Felicity laughed. 'Nice to see you,' she said. She watched as Henry climbed down the steps cut into the harbour wall. A nice man she thought, I must invite him and his wife for a meal. She was tired and really wanted to be tucked up in bed but having sat at her desk all day she felt obliged to have a little fresh air and exercise.

She was just beginning to walk along the wharf again when she heard Henry's voice.

'Felicity, are you still there? Come quickly.'

She stopped in her tracks, turned round and went back to the steps which Henry had taken. They were difficult in the dark and she stumbled, landing heavily on the sand. 'Henry,' she called out, 'where are you?'

'Over here.'

Henry and Archie were standing over a tiny shape pressed into the harbour wall.

'What is it,' Felicity said nervously, 'what have you found?'

'It's a girl,' Henry said, 'a young girl, she's terrified. I thought maybe you could reassure her.'

Felicity moved forward and knelt down beside the shape which gradually, as her eyes acclimatised, she recognised to be a very young girl. She had a tumble of dark hair, her knees were bought up to her chest, her arms wrapped round them for protection, her eyes were wide and scared. She was shaking but whether from cold or fright, Felicity could not tell. Tentatively she reached out and put her hand on her arm. The girl flinched.

'It's OK,' Felicity said, 'are you English?'

The girl shook her head.

'Polish,' Felicity said, remembering all the Polish flower pickers that had been down in Cornwall earlier in the year.

'No, Romania,' the girl said.

'Romanian!' Alarm bells sounded in Felicity's head. She turned quickly to Henry. 'This girl could be in danger,' she said, 'I think we need to get her back to my house and I need to ring the Chief Inspector in charge of the Irving case.'

It took a lot of reassurance to persuade Anya to

stand up and come with Felicity. Henry and Archie gallantly escorted them the short distance to Jericho Cottage and once at the door Felicity thanked him.

'We'll be alright now,' she said.

'Are you sure?'

Felicity nodded, anxious to get the girl inside and safe. She led her upstairs to the kitchen, sat her down at the table while she put on the kettle, then smiling at her reassuringly she dialled Keith's mobile number. He responded immediately.

'I'm sorry to trouble you,' Felicity said, 'are you asleep?'

'No, no I'm out walking the dog,' said Keith, 'perfect timing. What's up?'

'I have a Romanian girl here. I found her on the beach, she doesn't speak any English, she's clearly terrified. She is very, very young, much younger than Marianna I should think. She may have nothing to do with the case but …'

'So where is she now?' Keith interrupted.

'She's at my cottage.'

'Right, I'll be straight over.'

'Wait,' said Felicity, 'it's really late. She's absolutely exhausted and where will you take her? You can't lock her up in a cell. Wouldn't it be better if she stays with me and you come over first thing in the morning?'

'Do you mind doing that?'

'No, no not at all,' said Felicity.

'She might not be what she seems, maybe she'll

steal from you or cause trouble.'

'I'll take that risk,' said Felicity, 'I'll be careful and I'll make sure I don't lose her.'

'The Bishop of Truro is playing host to a Romanian priest at the moment,' Keith said.

'Good Heavens,' said Felicity, 'how do you know a thing like that?'

'I was at a dinner last night with the bishop, we were talking about the Irving case and he mentioned that he had this man staying with him, pleasant chap apparently, he could be a perfect interpreter. I'll get something laid on and send a car over at what, about eight?'

'That would be fine,' said Felicity.

'Any problems call me, yes?'

'I will,' she said. 'No news of Miles, I suppose?'

'None,' he said.

The girl was pathetically grateful. Felicity made her a cup of tea and scrambled eggs on toast, then ran a bath for her and indicated the spare room where her daughter Mel usually slept. She found an old pair of Mel's pyjamas, which swamped her and established her name was Anya. They shook hands formally on exchanging names. Anya smiled and nodded but her eyes kept darting to the front door and to the windows, as though she was expecting someone at any moment.

'Don't worry,' Felicity assured her. She took the

keys and going to the front door made a great play of locking it. Anya smiled properly for the first time. Then going into Mel's bedroom, Felicity showed her the window was locked and pulled the curtains. 'Safe,' Felicity said, hopefully.

She couldn't settle long after Anya was asleep. She ranged around the kitchen trying to make sense of it all. That the girl was linked to the Irving case, she had no doubt, not just because she was Romanian, but because she was so clearly terrified. She recognised that terror, it was the same terror Marianna had felt shortly before her death. It was after one o'clock when finally she tiptoed downstairs, checked the girl was asleep, then gave in herself to a few hours' fitful sleeping.

Over coffee and toast the next morning Felicity tried to explain to Anya that a policeman was coming to collect her. Felicity was anxious about a police car whisking her away and had decided she would offer to go too, to give the girl reassurance. All this proved unnecessary. At eight o'clock there was a ring on her bell and Chief Inspector Penrose was there in person, accompanied by a merry looking man in a black cassock and a long beard who was introduced as Father Adrian. They all sat together around Felicity's tiny kitchen table while she brewed yet more coffee. She was proud of Anya, although she looked tiny and vulnerable, she seemed to recognise she was in safe hands and was clearly anxious to cooperate.

Father Adrian began. 'Keith,' he said, 'let me just talk to Anya without interpreting for a few minutes, just to reassure her and explain who I am and who you are and that we are here to help her and that she is in no trouble.' A long discussion followed, Father Adrian speaking at great speed with Anya occasionally replying in a tiny, timid voice. She found it difficult to meet anyone's eyes and tended to speak by addressing the tabletop. Now and again she twisted her hands in her lap.

At long last Father Adrian stopped and turned to Keith. 'I have explained to Anya that I am now going to translate what she has told me.' His face was grave, the twinkle in his eye had quite gone. 'Anya is a, how do you call it, a sex worker. She is only about sixteen, she is not too sure of her age because she was an orphanage child and no birthdays were celebrated. She was brought to England believing that she would have work as a domestic servant instead of which it was the usual story – raped and beaten until she agreed to be a prostitute.'

'How long has she been in the country?' Keith asked, his voice was grim.

'Since the turn of the year, they came over just after Christmas.'

'They?'

'She, two other girls and Marianna, her friend, the girl who died in the Irvings' house.'

'So she knew Marianna?' Keith asked.

'Oh yes, Marianna was very kind to her, looked after her, was like a mother to her she said.'

'Does she realise Marianna is dead?'

'Most certainly – that is why she is here.'

Keith frowned. 'For what reason, what was she hoping to find?'

'She was not hoping to find anything,' said Father Adrian, 'she is a simple girl, not stupid, but I think there is a tendency for her to think in straight lines. Her only friend is dead, she is sure that the man who acted as their pimp killed her. She needed to get away from him and she needed to tell someone her suspicions. She wants Marianna's killer to be punished.'

'Couldn't she have just gone to a policeman in London?'

'In London she was afraid, afraid Steve would find her. Marianna had told her all about her planned journey to St Ives, they had rehearsed it together, so Anya simply did the same thing, following her friend's footsteps, thinking there would be someone down here who would know Marianna's story and she could tell them hers.'

'Well, in that,' said Keith, 'she was right. It amazes me that she found her way to St Ives, with no ticket and no language.'

'She made one mistake,' said Father Adrian. 'She did not change trains at St Erth, she stayed on the train until Penzance.'

'So how did she get to St Ives from Penzance?'

Keith asked, intrigued.

'She says a kind man gave her a lift when he saw her crying outside the station,' said Father Adrian. Then seeing Keith's expression, he added hastily. 'I think he was just that, Keith, a kind man. She seems most grateful to him.'

'Could you ask Anya how Marianna knew about the Irvings and where to find them.'

There was a short exchange of conversation. This time Anya was more animated. She finds it easier to talk about Marianna than herself, Felicity thought.

The suddenly, Anya began to cry. Felicity jumped up and reached for a box of tissues. She sat beside her on the sofa, slipped an arm around her and gave her a hug. 'What is it?' she asked Father Adrian.

'She is very sad about the death of her friend.'

There was a movement from the old armchair. Orlando tottered to his feet, jumped down heavily and then with a huge effort jumped up onto Anya's lap. The girl, started with surprise, and then laughed. She stroked Orlando who settled down on her lap. Her tears forgotten now, she spoke rapidly to Father Adrian.

'She says he is a beautiful cat but very fat.'

'That's true,' Felicity admitted.

'She also says that the animals in St Ives have been very kind to her.'

Keith frowned. 'What on earth does she mean by that?'

Felicity smiled. 'You surely can guess who found Anya last night.'

'I assumed it was you.'

'I was there, certainly, but the person who brought Anya to my attention was Archie.'

'Archie?'

'The dog who found Sir Hugo's abandoned board bag.'

'Oh, that Archie – fairly hideous curly haired Archie, with attitude.'

'With a noble soul,' Felicity corrected, firmly.

Their smiles vanished as quickly as they had come. The story they were hearing was too horrible to be side-tracked, for more than a moment. They talked on. Gradually, carefully, Keith extracted, as near as he could, the location of where Steve was keeping the girls. It sounded like Paddington, for it was only a few minutes walk from the station.

'If you'll excuse me I'm going to make some phone calls,' he said. 'This Steve is likely to move the girls again now Anya has run away too. I think we need to act quickly.' He returned ten minutes later. 'The Met are on the job,' he said, 'they think they may already know this Steve. How are we doing here?'

'We've just been hearing Anya's life story,' said Felicity, her eyes bright with tears. 'She was in an orphanage until she was fourteen, though not the same one as Marianna. She ran away, ended up on the streets of Bucharest and became a prostitute almost immediately. It was the only way she could feed herself. It was there that she met Marianna who helped her, taught her the basic instincts of survival and it was Marianna who learnt about a chance of coming to England. She had found out about her brother, who she had never forgotten. She had known he had been adopted by an English couple because she had seen the Irvings in the orphanage and a friend of hers – I suspect it was a client – was a judge. He checked the court records for her and found the name of the adoptive parents. Apparently Marianna was obsessed with wanting to find her brother and so the chance of going to England was ideal. Steve promised them good jobs over here, looking after children, cleaning houses for rich people in London. Anya, Marianna and two other girls were all flown over to Heathrow, they were taken to a house where they were raped and beaten by Steve and several other men. Since then they have been prisoners. Steve feeds them and buys their clothes. They are, Anya says, 'like animals in a zoo.'

'So how did Marianna find out about her brother?' Keith asked.

'One of Marianna's clients left a newspaper behind him and there on the front page was the story of Sir Hugo's disappearance and Marianna realised immediately that the family concerned was the family she was seeking. Ever since then she has been plotting to escape. Anya is convinced that Steve followed her and killed her.'

'But how did Steve know where to go?' Keith

asked.

Father Adrian interrupted. 'I asked that question. Apparently some evenings when things were quiet, Steve would fill the girls full of drink and drugs and sometimes they would talk. Marianna got angry with Steve and told him she had a rich brother who would save her one day and told him the whole story. When she disappeared he knew exactly where she had gone and he had to silence her.'

A plan was hatched. Anya would be taken to Truro and placed in the care of Social Services. Father Adrian was in Cornwall for another week and during that time he would keep a watching brief over her and help her by interpreting where necessary.

'What will become of her?' Felicity said. She and Keith were standing by her front door. Father Adrian walking ahead with Anya, talking animatedly explaining what was happening.

Keith let out a sigh. 'Well I suppose she'll be deported,' and then seeing the stricken expression on Felicity's face added, 'once she is well and has her strength back, and of course not until she's testified, if we get to court. It won't happen for some time.'

'She's so young,' Felicity said, 'sixteen, hardly started. I hope they get that bastard who did this to her and to Marianna.'

'They will,' said Keith, 'but there are so many others like him. Assuming he is Marianna's killer and he must be, I'm pretty sure we have his DNA. She'd clawed at his face before she died, poor girl. It's a wonderful thing DNA, and I should think there's little doubt we'll get him.'

10

'Just because God Almighty Chief Inspector Penrose says you've got to jump, it doesn't mean you have to. Why is it you, who have to go to London, why can't he?'

Jack Curnow let out a theatrical sigh, turned his back on his wife and began brewing a pot of tea. He swirled the hot water around in the teapot unnecessarily vigorously, keeping anger only just at bay.

'Well, answer me then,' Maggie said.

'There's nothing to answer. It is my job and I have to go – that's all there is to it, Maggie.'

'He treats you like some sort of errand boy. Why can't he do his own trips to London?'

'Actually,' said Jack, 'he's been to London twice in the last ten days but tomorrow is all about paperwork. I'm going to catch the sleeper and I'll be home at teatime tomorrow.'

'If it's just paperwork, why don't they just e-mail it or fax it, why do you have to deliver it, it's a ridiculous waste of public money.'

Jack sighed again. 'Look, we've already been through this several times. The Met have got the guy who murdered the girl in St Ives. His name is Steve Jackson and he's wanted up there for a whole series of revolting crimes – imprisonment, living off immoral earnings, rape and a whole bunch of sex and drug crimes – it is more sensible that he's charged up there not down here. Normally he would be brought back to Cornwall to be charged for the murder. I have to take all the paperwork up and go through everything with the Met to make sure that we've really got the bastard. It's a big responsibility. Men like him are the scum of the earth and they need to be behind bars. We've got to make sure there is no slip up.' He rounded on his wife suddenly. 'You should be grateful.'

'Grateful!' Maggie roared, 'grateful for what? Grateful for having my husband at the beck and call of the Force all the time, always putting his job before me and the baby.'

'Yes, you should be grateful,' Jack said, 'grateful that there is a police force to make sure that men like Jackson will be locked up, grateful too that you didn't have to lead a life like Marianna or Anya.'

'Grateful I'm not a whore – thanks a bunch, Jack Curnow! You do have a nice turn of phrase. If you do have to go up to London why do you have to go up on the sleeper, why can't you just go up and back in the day?'

'Because I won't have enough time to get the work done I need to do. Now will you drop it.'

'It's you I'm more likely to drop. I've had enough of this Jack, I really have.'

'Well that, Maggie, is entirely up to you. I'm going out.' He slammed the teapot down and headed for the door.

'Where?' she screamed after him.

'None of your damn business.'

'I thought I had sent you home for the day?' Keith said as Jack put his head around the door of Keith's office.

'I thought I'd come back and see if there is anything I could do.'

Keith looked at him and frowned. 'Trouble at home?'

Jack nodded. 'Another ear-wigging.'

'What about this time?'

'Going up to London.'

Keith let out a sigh and put down his pen. 'So what's wrong with you going up to London, Jack?'

'Well, as you know, absolutely nothing, sir, it's just she's got this bee in her bonnet, she doesn't like me being away. I don't know what to make of it.'

'Would it help if I went to see her?'

Jack looked at his boss, doubtfully. 'I don't know. She's not best fond of you, sir, she seems to think it's all your fault.'

Keith laughed. 'Well my back is broad and of course she's right, it is all my fault. If I can find the time, Jack, I'll pop in and see if I can straighten her out.'

'Oh, I wouldn't do that,' Jack began.

'It's alright. When I say straighten her out I'll be nothing but sweetness and light, I promise. Maybe I should get Barbara to have a word with her too, that might help.'

'Yes, it might,' Jack admitted, 'thank you. Anything new?'

Keith shook his head. 'Miles Irving seems to have disappeared off the face of the earth just like his father. Are the two connected, Jack, what do you think?'

Jack advanced into the room, shut the door and sat down on the only available chair, having first removed a dusty pile of files.

'Does Lady Irving think her husband is dead?' Jack asked.

Keith nodded. 'Yes, I think so. I don't know what to make of that woman now, I liked her to start with. Now, well, I'm not sure, I do. I hate the way she deceived Miles. I think she feels about Hugo much as we do. Initially she couldn't believe it, he was such a good surfer etc, etc, but when he didn't come home she started to believe there must have been an accident. She reckons he had a stroke or a heart attack.'

'Then why was there no body?' Jack asked.

'There isn't sometimes, the body gets trapped under water. The harbourmaster says by nine days the body should reappear if it sinks at the time of death, but it didn't. Maybe it was swept out to sea, any number of things could happen. Finding no body when the sea is involved doesn't mean anything, we know that. We've come across that before over the years. The harbourmaster reckons what is left of Sir Hugo could be half way to America by now.'

'Then if he died in a freak accident,' said Jack, 'there is no reason to assume that his death has anything at all to do with his son's disappearance. What does Lady Irving think of Miles going missing?'

'Hard to tell,' said Keith, 'we didn't get on that well last time we met.'

'Perhaps you should get Mrs Penrose on it again. She was right about Jackson, he is a dead ringer for her identikit picture, apparently.'

'That'll teach you non-believers,' Keith said, with a smile. 'I told you guys she needed to be taken seriously.'

'Then why not ask her to have a think about Miles?'

Keith shook his head. 'That's not what she does. It's places that do it for her, largely I think. She certainly can't conjure up ideas as to where somebody has disappeared, particlarly someone she has never met.'

'She found George Gresham.'

'That was different again,' said Keith. 'She had a relationship with the family, she cared passionately about him and them. She was also a schoolteacher remember; she has a natural gift for guessing how children will think and react. She was emotionally involved with that case right up to her neck. This is very different. She has never met Miles, she knows next to nothing about him other than his sad past. She has absolutely nothing to go on and nor, sadly, do we. We still don't even know that he came to St Ives at all that day.'

'Somebody let Marianna into that house,' said Jack, 'someone with a key and we're confident it wasn't Jenny the housekeeper so who else could it be?'

'It wasn't Lady Irving either, she has an alibi for that night, I've checked it out and it stands up, she was at dinner with friends. So the only other two people with keys are Miles and his father, both of whom are missing. What a mess.'

'Well at least we know now that Miles wasn't the murderer, that's something,' said Jack.

'Assuming the DNA comes right, though I'm sure it will,' Keith agreed. 'So what have we got – Miles's disappearance is unconnected with his father's because his father's was a freak accident, right?' Jack nodded. 'He didn't disappear because he killed his sister, Jackson did that, right?' Again, Jack nodded. 'Whatever happened to make him disappear happened after his conversation with me. When I made the appointment to see him, he seemed genuinely pleased to be meeting me and doing something to help. I think he quite liked the responsibility. I don't know, I'm guessing, but I think he was pleased to be helping his mother and pleased to be seen as being able to. There was no reluctance about coming to Cornwall and no reluctance at all about meeting me, quite the contrary.'

'So we're back full circle,' said Jack, 'the only obvious thing that could have made Miles go AWOL was meeting the sister he didn't know he had,'

'Or,' said Keith, 'coming across her dead body in his hall.'

'Or,' said Jack, 'both.'

The flight to Tresco was glorious. Last time Felicity had made the trip the weather had been quite overcast but this morning the sun was beating relentlessly out of a clear blue sky. She craned her neck out of the window watching Penzance slip away followed by the fabulous coastline – and then inland over fields like pocket handkerchiefs and finally Land's End. The mainland behind them, Scilly beckoned. She had booked herself in for two nights at the Island Hotel, which she could not afford. She had persuaded herself that in season for such a short stay there was no alternative, which was true, and that by booking herself into the least expensive room she was actually saving money which, of course, was untrue.

After dropping her bags at the hotel Felicity picked up her art things and went to hire a bike for a couple of days. She then set off for the Abbey Garden. She knew the garden would be very busy at this time of year, but she had made arrangements with the curator, to be shown the plants she wanted and within an hour, easel propped up in the shade, she was hard at work, mercifully well away from the walkways and almost camouflaged from sight.

The garden never failed to inspire her. It was like being picked up and dropped into some far off country, Peru perhaps. She knew there were over five thousand different kinds of exotic plants in the Abbey Garden, which was not difficult to believe. More extraordinary was how the balance of colour and size made the plants seem at home, even though most had their origins half a world away. It was crazy to think this exotic world had been created in part of the UK. After nearly three hours solid work the heat had started to get to her. She had long ago finished her bottle of water and she was starting to feel uncomfortably hot and sweaty. She had laid down the colours she needed and decided to go to the café for a drink, something to eat and a much needed trip to the loo. She was busy packing up her easel and paints when she saw him. He was on the path below where she was painting. She had a good view of him but he did not even glance in her direction, he was whistling something tuneless under his breath and appeared relaxed and unhurried. He was very close to her when he stopped and for a moment she thought he had spotted her, but it was simply to check a tap. He produced a spanner from his jacket pocket and began tightening it. The moment gave her the opportunity to study his face in profile from what was no more than six metres away. He was the spitting image of Sir Hugo in every detail – same build, same face, same grey hair except for the ponytail. It was this sudden realisation of what was wrong with the ponytail, which made Felicity almost gasp aloud.

By early evening she was back at the hotel and before changing for dinner she put through a telephone call to Truro.

'I've seen him again,' she told Keith Penrose without preamble.

'Who?'

'The Sir Hugo look-alike. I'm on Tresco, sorry, I should have explained, I'm here for a few days painting.'

'Alright for some,' Keith grumbled.

'Jealousy is a wasted emotion, Chief Inspector,' she said in her best prim school m'am manner.

'And do you think it is Sir Hugo?' Keith asked, wearily.

'No,' said Felicity, 'that's just it, it can't be and I've suddenly realised why.'

'And are you willing to share this invaluable piece of knowledge with me?' Keith asked.

'It's the ponytail, I've suddenly realised that in the time since he disappeared, Sir Hugo couldn't possibly have grown it. There isn't five months of growth there, more like five years. It goes half way down his back.'

'It could be a wig, I suppose.'

'Believe me, it couldn't,' said Felicity, 'it's too dreadful, it couldn't be anything but the real thing, truly.'

'So that puts paid to our one and only lead on Sir Hugo,' said Keith.

'Yes,' Felicity agreed, 'though it is strange – in every other respect, except for the hair, he is a dead ringer, identical. Sir Hugo didn't have a brother, did he?'

'No,' said Keith, 'no siblings at all. He was bought up in Yorkshire, the only child of a miner. All that sort of thing was checked out at the time of his disappearance, friends, family, everything.'

'Then it's all very odd because put this chap in a suit, cut his hair and he would be Sir Hugo.'

'Why not talk to him,' Keith suggested, 'I would have thought the task would appeal to your naturally inquisitive nature.'

Felicity ignored the jibe. 'And say what?'

'Say he gave you quite a turn because he looks so like Sir Hugo Irving, a friend of yours who disappeared and then just see what comes out.'

'Alright,' said Felicity, 'I will. It can't do any harm unless, of course, he is Sir Hugo in which case, if I haven't rung you in twenty-four hours assume I am somewhere in the garden with a pitchfork through the heart.'

'Not funny,' said Keith, 'incidentally, we've got

Jackson. His DNA was found under the fingernails of Marianna and he has all but confessed, he completely caved in apparently. It's odd really you wouldn't think someone capable of such truly hideous crimes would be such an easy nut to crack.'

'Bullies are always cowards at heart,' Felicity said. She hesitated, she wanted to ask about Anya but her courage failed her.

The next morning full of inquisitive zeal, Felicity headed early for the Abbey Garden. The bike ride was wonderful. It was a stunning morning, the sea like glass, the sun already beating down high in the sky. Scilly on a good day was such an assault on the senses, the extraordinary blues and greens of the sea, the wonderful smells of the flowers combined with the tanginess of the seaweed, the sense of being on the very edge of the earth, with nothing between the islands and America.

By the time she reached the garden, Felicity was full of optimism and purpose, her head spinning from the beauty all round her. It was a blow to find that it was closed until late morning. A film crew were in residence and until they had finished filming, all visitors were banned. It was explained that visitors could not be expected to be quiet and Felicity was just trying to convince the woman serving her coffee that she would make no noise at all when a voice called out her name. It belonged to a pretty young woman sitting at a table surrounded by paperwork. The girl looked to be in her mid-twenties with short curly hair and the well-scrubbed healthy complexion of someone who spent most of her life outside.

'Mrs Paradise,' she said, 'I heard you were painting some of the plants in the garden for a book, is that right?'

Felicity bought her mug of coffee over to the girl's table. 'Yes, that's right,' she said.

The girl moved her papers aside to make room. 'I'd love to see them if you've got the time.'

Felicity sat down with a rueful smile. 'I've certainly got time,' she grumbled, 'two hours to kill, in fact.'

'I'm sorry, we should have let you know about the film crew yesterday.'

'That's OK, I'm not really grumpy. Tell me are you lucky enough to work here?'

The girl nodded. 'Sort of, my name is Sarah Cunningham. I'm studying horticulture at the Duchy but I'm doing work experience here and on St Michael's Mount. I saw you working on the Mount a week or two ago but I didn't like to disturb you.'

'I wish everybody had your degree of tact,' said Felicity, with a smile.

'It's odd,' Sarah agreed, 'visitors never leave artists alone to work.' Felicity produced her sketches and the two women studied them. 'They are very good. I like this one of the agave plant, you're very clever.'

'Thank you,' said Felicity, 'I'm struggling really. Plants aren't normally what I draw. Are you enjoying being here?'

Sarah smiled. 'Loving it, I've got another two weeks on Tresco and then I'm back on the Mount until the new term starts. I just love the whole thing, the plants of course, this garden which is magnificent, but also island life. I'm hoping there might be a job here for me when I qualify.'

'You're very young,' said Felicity, 'wouldn't you find life on Scilly a bit restrictive.'

Sarah shook her head. 'I don't think so, it suits me somehow.'

Looking at her bright-eyed enthusiasm Felicity tended to agree. There was a pause in the conversation, Felicity sipped her coffee and an idea suddenly came to her. 'There's a man who works in the garden, I wonder if you know him?'

Sarah smiled. 'There're a lot of people working here.'

'I realise that. This chap is fairly distinctive though. He's in his mid fifties I would say with a ponytail.'

'Oh, you mean Bob,' said Sarah.

'Bob,' repeated Felicity.

'Yes,' said Sarah, 'Bob Barnes. He is an odd character, very reclusive, just gets on with his work. He is a maintenance man and has a cottage at New Grimsby. He lives alone, nobody knows him very well, as far as I know.'

'Has he been working at the Abbey Garden long?' Felicity asked, her heart quickening in anticipation of Sarah's reply.

'Oh yes, for years. He's an institution,' said Sarah.

'Are you sure?' Felicity asked.

'Yes, I'm quite sure,' Sarah said, curiously, 'why do you want to know?'

'He just reminds me of someone I knew,' Felicity said, hurriedly, 'but he can't be that person if he's worked here for years.'

'I can't tell you how many,' said Sarah, 'but a good long time.'

'And certainly a lot longer than just this season?' Felicity asked.

'Oh yes, I did work experience here last year as well and he was definitely here then.'

Blast thought Felicity, well that's the end of my theory that Sir Hugo could have gone native on Tresco. Two coffees later the film crew were done and she was let into the Garden. By three o'clock she had everything she needed and headed back to the Island Hotel where she e-mailed Chief Inspector Penrose.

Sir Hugo look-alike, just that, she typed, *real name Bob Barnes. Lived and worked on Tresco for some years, apparently, if you want to check him out. Sorry wild goose chase culminating in dead end.*

On the same evening that Felicity was flying

back to Penzance from Tresco, Chief Inspector Keith Penrose arrived home in a thoroughly bad temper. The Irving case was becoming more and more uncomfortable. Until the discovery of Marianna Ivanovitch's body in the Irvings' holiday home, the disappearance of Sir Hugo Irving was more or less a closed case. When Sir Hugo had first disappeared, the case had attracted a lot of high profile interest, questions were asked by the very top brass in the police force and Keith had felt under considerable pressure to produce some results. Gradually, though, when firstly no body appeared and secondly exhaustive enquiries proved that Sir Hugo had no apparent reason for either wanting himself dead or missing, both the press and more importantly, his superintendent, accepted that what had happened had to have been a tragic accident. The meeting with Miles, which never took place, was supposed to bring that case to a natural conclusion.

Now the press were having a field day – Miles's adoption, his dead sister a prostitute, sex and murder a powerful combination. The press were firmly of the view that the disappearance of Sir Hugo had to be linked in some way to the subsequent events. Keith could not see how, but at the same time what unquestionably linked the two events was the fact that both father and son seemed to have disappeared off the face of the earth. Were they dead? Had they gone missing independently of one another or had Miles gone to join his father somewhere for some unimaginable reason? This was of course what the press were endlessly speculating upon, and in order to whip up interest and sell newspapers, they were definitely going for a conspiracy story. What was absolutely clear though was that everyone concerned wanted results and a result was something Keith seemed incapable of delivering. The e-mail from Mrs Paradise had been the final straw. He had been clutching at straws, he knew, but because she had such an uncanny way of getting to the bottom of things, he had hoped against hope that the strange pony-tailed man on Tresco was indeed Sir Hugo Irving. Now it was clear he was not. It was ludicrous, a case that was filling pages of newsprint had not one single tangible lead.

Barbara was at the kitchen sink peeling potatoes. 'You're home early,' she said.

'I'll go away again then if I'm in the way,' said Keith.

'Oh, for Heaven's sake,' she said, 'what's wrong with you?'

'Sorry, sorry,' he said, 'I'll put the kettle on.'

Tea made they sat down at the kitchen table together. Barbara was a well-preserved woman for her fifty-three years. She had allowed her hair to go grey and it suited her. She had typically Cornish colouring – despite her dark hair she had a fresh, fair complexion and most arresting bright blue eyes. She had been a very pretty girl and, although considerably overweight, she was now a handsome woman, though formidable. She dressed severely in power suits as befitting her position on the Planning Committee. She was a good woman, but not very cosy and definitely lacking in any serious sense of humour or fun. For some reason these days, being in her company made Keith feel tired.

'So what's eating you then?' she asked.

'This Irving case,' he shook his head, 'I'm getting nowhere.'

'Well you certainly better get somewhere soon the amount of attention you're attracting. My friends keep badgering me to know what's going on. Is the super giving you a hard time?'

Keith nodded. 'Everyone is giving me a hard time and I have got absolutely no leads. I don't know whether the disappearances of the father and son are linked or not, I don't know whether their disappearances have anything to do with poor Marianna, I just don't know what to make of it all.'

'Forget the father,' said Barbara, 'you weren't able to turn up anything on him, and you've had months to do that. Concentrate on the son before the trail goes cold on him. The father probably did drown, certainly the evidence suggests he did, but there's nothing to suggest the son died, he has to be somewhere.'

Keith looked at her in surprise. 'Yes, you're right,' he said.

'Take me through the story again,' Barbara said.

Keith began a quick resume. Barbara listened in silence. When he had finished Barbara looked at him quizzically. 'So your Mrs Paradise seems to feature again. She pops up like a bad penny, doesn't she, whenever you have a difficult case?'

Keith nodded. 'She's been most helpful actually, I don't think we'd have found it so easy to nail Jackson without her help. She certainly put us on the right track.'

'Pretty is she?' Barbara asked.

Keith let out a sigh. 'I can assure you,' he said, 'there is absolutely no reason for you to be jealous of Felicity Paradise.'

'Who said anything about jealous,' said Barbara, 'don't flatter yourself. I'm just interested in your relationship. You seem to think a lot of her.'

'Felicity Paradise would not be interested in a chap like me, nor is she the sort of person who would mess about with a married man and in any event, I have been faithful to you since the day we married, and always will be.'

'Just checking,' said Barbara.

'Right, with your check completed, have you got anything else to say on the matter?'

'Well, I'd have thought it was obvious,' said Barbara.

'What's obvious?' said Keith.

'In fact I can't think why your precious Mrs Paradise hasn't thought of it herself. I'd understand a man not seeing what Miles would do, but I'd have thought your Mrs Paradise would have worked it out, her and her second sight.'

Keith sighed. 'Barbara, if you've got anything to say could you just say it, I'm so tired.'

'Well, as I said,' Barbara said, 'it's obvious. The boy, Miles, gets told he's adopted. Even if he didn't see the body of his sister, the publicity will mean he now knows she's dead. It's obvious what he would do in the circumstances.'

'I wish you'd stop saying it's obvious, it's not at all obvious to me,' said Keith.

'Well it certainly is to me,' said Barbara, 'what I'd do if I was Miles Irving is go to Romania to discover the roots I didn't know I had until a couple of weeks ago.'

Keith stared at his wife. 'My God,' he said, 'you're right, of course you're right, why on earth didn't we think of that.' He jumped to his feet, seized his wife's head between his hands and kissed the top of it. 'God bless you, dear,' he said. He drained his cup and was out of the kitchen door before she had a chance to reply.

11

Felicity was having a great deal of difficulty getting hold of Chief Inspector Keith Penrose, he wasn't answering his mobile, he wasn't at the station and nobody would say where he'd gone, it was all very frustrating. In the end she was forced to leave a message confirming the contents of her e-mail. She would have liked to discuss her findings on Tresco with him but he, like the Irvings, seemed to have disappeared.

In fact, with a few hours to kill having booked his flight to Bucharest, Keith was sitting in the rather austere kitchen in Jack Curnow's house drinking coffee with Jack's wife, Maggie. Maggie had been flustered by Keith's sudden appearance at her front door and they had not got off to a good start.

'He's not here,' Maggie said rudely on answering the front door, 'he's at work, you should know that.'

'I do know that,' Keith replied evenly, 'it's you I've come to see.'

Her face paled. 'What's wrong, has he been hurt?'

'No, no he's fine, he's sitting at his desk in the station. Look Maggie, I don't want to stand on the doorstep all day. Are you going to invite me in for a cup of coffee, I just need to have a chat with you?'

While Maggie made the coffee Keith's attempts at small talk fell on stony ground. It was a shame. She was a pretty girl, slightly overweight, but in an attractive way with natural blonde hair and a beautiful skin. When she smiled, which didn't seem likely at the moment, Keith knew attractive dimples appeared in either cheek. At the moment she looked solemn and very fed up. Having congratulated her on the fact that she was pregnant, he enquired how she was feeling, to be told she felt sick as a dog most of the time, thank you very much. At last she came and sat beside him, a cup of coffee for him, an orange juice for her.

'So why are you here?' She asked.

'I am aware,' said Keith, carefully, 'that you are not very happy with Jack's job.'

'Has he been telling tales?'

'No,' said Keith, firmly, 'but Jack's been my sergeant now for some years and we've got to know each other very well. I am aware that he is worried and unhappy about your attitude to his job.' Maggie started to protest. Keith held up a hand to silence her. 'Let me finish,' he said. 'Don't think for one moment that I'm not sympathetic about how you feel. Barbara has had many difficulties over the years with my career and many coppers' wives will say the same.'

'If they stay around long enough to be able to tell you,' said Maggie. 'The divorce rate between policemen and their wives is among one of the highest in the country.'

'I'm aware of that,' said Keith, 'but Barbara and I have been married for thirty-two years and I know quite a few like us. Jack is devoted to you, he really wants you to be happy.'

'I just want him to have an ordinary job,' said Maggie, 'something like my brother.'

'What does your brother do?' Keith asked.

'He's a painter and decorator, he's in partnership with a friend from school, they have a really good little business and he's home for tea every day at five o'clock and he leaves for work every day at eight and his wife knows where he is and there's a routine and it's not dangerous or stressful.'

Keith picked his words carefully.

'It's not a very exciting job though, is it?' he said. 'Same old thing day after day, just a different house, a different colour. Your husband is a clever lad, he can go a long way in the police force with your support. You know this case we're dealing with, the Irvings?'

'How could I not,' said Maggie, 'turn on the television, open the newspaper, it's all over the place.'

'Right,' said Keith, 'father and son are missing, yes.'

'Yes, it's all very odd,' Maggie conceded.

'Your husband found the son this morning.'

'He did?'

Keith nodded. 'He's staying in the Inter-Continental Hotel in Bucharest, I'm on my way there now when I finish talking to you.'

Maggie's eyes widened. 'Is Jack going with you?'

'No, he's not, he's staying here.'

'That's good, where is Bucharest anyway?'

'Romania.'

'Isn't that where Count Dracula comes from?'

Keith smiled. 'I rather think it is,' he agreed.

'So my Jack's found Miles Irving?'

'He certainly has and in a couple of days the newspapers will be full of it and you'll know it was down to your husband that the boy has been found. You should be proud.'

'I am but I still hate it – police work is dangerous work,' Maggie was aggressive.

'Maggie, life is dangerous,' said Keith, 'please God it will never happen, but your brother could fall off his ladder. If Jack worked in London he could be on a tube train blown up by terrorists, if he was a salesman driving around the country he could be in a motorway pile up. Once you're out of the womb, life is dangerous.' Seeing Maggie's expression Keith cursed himself. 'Sorry, that was not a particularly tactful way of putting things to you at the moment, but all I'm trying to say is we can't completely protect ourselves or our loved ones from danger. Look at the case Jack and I had back in February – that poor girl subject of a hit and run in Lemon Street. One minute she's alive, the next dead, all because of a couple of drunken youths from up-country. Most of Jack's day is spent either at his desk or interviewing people who will do him absolutely no harm at all. Now and again things do get a bit dodgy but this is Cornwall not Brixton. The death of Marianna Ivanovitch is so shocking to us all because nothing like that has ever happened in living memory in St Ives, or anywhere else in West Cornwall come to that.' He hesitated; at least she was listening. 'You know what I would recommend. I know you have your part-time reception job at the dentist's but maybe you need to get out more, Maggie, with your friends.'

'I don't have any friends,' said Maggie, 'I don't come from round here, remember.'

'Ah,' said Keith, 'but that's all going to change isn't it, now you're pregnant.'

'I don't see how,' said Maggie.

'Antenatal classes, mother and toddler groups, I promise you, Maggie, by this time next year you'll have a ton of friends – that's what having children does for you.'

The dimples suddenly appeared and changed her completely – she really was very pretty. 'You seem to know a lot about it, Chief Inspector.'

'I do have a couple of kids of my own,' Keith said, 'most of the friends Barbara has today are the mothers of children who were friends with our kids, friends she's had for thirty years, some of them are grannies

131

now …' he hesitated. 'Don't you and Jack ever go out with any of his colleagues? He's has a couple of good pals on the Force, both are married I know.'

'We do occasionally,' Maggie admitted, 'but it's the same old thing, everybody's hours are irregular so trying to plan anything is so hard.'

'Then my advice would be,' said Keith, 'to make a life for yourself, establish your own social life, your own routine and now and again, if Jack comes home and you're not here, well, that's tough – he might even have to learn to cook his own supper. It would do him good not to have you at his beck and call. Having said that, stick with him, Maggie. He's a good man, a clever chap and will be a wonderful father to your child, and in my view a good loving husband to you now and in the future.'

Maggie looked down at her hands. 'You think I've been too harsh on him?'

'I think you have,' Keith admitted, 'but I understand why, or at least I think I do. It is tough being a policeman's wife, but once you get used to it, accept his mad hours and crazy goings on and just get on with your own life, you might find things are a lot more fun than the routine of home for tea at five and followed by an evening of the telly.'

'Thanks for spending the time to come and see me,' Maggie said. 'I will do my best to support him. Did he really find Miles Irving?'

'Yes,' said Keith, 'he really did.'

Keith thought about the conversation as he was driving across Bodmin Moor. Never a fan of public transport, Keith found the Newquay flight to Stansted, followed by the transfer to Heathrow quite intolerable. Instead, he was driving direct to Heathrow and staying overnight with his sister near Reading on the way – cheaper on the public purse too.

It was not strictly true, of course, that Jack Curnow had found Miles but it was near enough the truth to serve the purpose. Following Barbara's suggestion, Keith had asked Jack to check out flights to Bucharest immediately following Marianna's death. Sure enough, the afternoon flight out of Heathrow on the day following the discovery of her body, Miles's name had appeared on the passenger list. Keith thought about it – all his life Miles must have been used to staying in the best hotels wherever he went. A quick check established that the Inter-Continental in Parliament Square was the most likely candidate and sure enough Jack was able to establish that Miles had indeed checked in there and appeared to be still staying in the hotel. The super was all for having Miles arrested and shipped back to the UK, presuming he was a key witness in a murder, but Keith had persuaded him that the best way to handle the boy was for him to go out and talk to Miles and hopefully bring him home.

'He's a sensitive lad who has experienced a

terrible shock. If we're to get his co-operation we're far more likely to succeed if we take the gently, gently approach.'

Surprisingly, given the acrimonious nature of their last meeting, Lady Irving had supported this view. Hugely relieved that her son was found, she felt Keith was the person to bring him home.

Keith was exhausted when at five o'clock Romanian time the following day, he found himself hurtling through the grim streets of Bucharest on his way from the airport to the hotel. It was stifling hot, something that had never occurred to him to expect, associating Romania in his mind with Russia. He felt miserably uncomfortable in his suit and thought longingly of a cold shower and an early night. He was very fond of his sister Betty. Unlike Keith she had followed on the family tradition of farming. She had met her husband, Ed, at agricultural college. They had married and Ed had landed a good job as an estate manager on a big estate in West Berkshire. They had worked hard, raised three children and had recently been able to buy a cottage on the edge of the estate so that they were all set for their retirement. It had been a very pleasant evening, Keith had spent an hour or so with Ed in the pub while Betty prepared supper, his nephews and niece had come and gone, the wine had flowed and it was after two by the time he and Betty had finally said goodnight. They saw each other so rarely there was so much to catch up on and they had always been close.

'When I retire,' Keith assured her, 'you'll be sick to death of the sight of me. I'll be here all the time, getting under your feet.'

'I'd like that very much, big bro,' she assured him, giving him a hug.

It had been a great evening but now the dull headache which had persisted all day had developed into a steady hammering behind the eyes. As it happened he was spared the need to go straight to work. Enquiries at reception established that Miles Irving was out for the evening and not expected back until late the hall porter assured him. There were no plans for Mr Irving to check out of the hotel on an immediate basis and armed with this welcome information, Keith did exactly what he needed to do and went to bed early.

The following morning Keith had no difficulty in picking out Miles from the rest of his fellow breakfast diners. His image, of course, had been splashed all over the paper in recent days but even without this Keith was sure he would have been able to identify him. He was dressed casually in jeans and a T-shirt; he looked very alone, out of place, absurdly young and vulnerable. Keith walked directly up to his table.

'Would you mind if I joined you?' he asked.

Miles looked startled. 'I'm sorry, do I know you?'

'We were due to meet just over two weeks ago,' said Keith, 'my name is Chief Inspector Keith Penrose.'

Miles looked hugely shocked and, if possible, even more vulnerable and overwhelmed. Then his good manners got the better of him and he stood up and held out his hand. 'Miles Irving,' he said and smiled slightly, 'but then obviously you know that.'

'So may I join you?' Keith said, returning the smile.

'Well, yes, of course.'

'So may I ask if you are having a fruitful time here?' Keith asked.

Miles shook his head. 'Not really. I'm trying to find out about my birth family, but then you must have guessed that. It's all pretty miserable actually; the bureaucratic wheels move very slowly over here and have to be oiled with constant 'donations'. Extracting information is really difficult and here I am in my country of birth and I can't even speak the language,' he shrugged his shoulders and looked down forlornly at his empty plate.

'So have you found out any of what you wanted to know?' Keith asked.

'Yes,' said Miles, he raised his huge haunted brown eyes to Keith's face, 'both my birth mother and father are dead. My mother died within a month of my birth but my father only died eighteen months ago. If the Irvings had told me the truth from the beginning, I would have at least have had an opportunity to meet him before he died, not to mention helping Marianna and avoiding her death altogether.'

'You sound very bitter,' Keith said.

'I am very bitter, wouldn't you be?'

Keith did not hesitate in his reply. 'Yes,' he said simply.

The two men drank coffee in silence for a moment.

'We need to talk,' said Keith, 'there's a lot of ground to cover. Any idea where we could do that, where you'd feel most comfortable?'

'There's a wonderful park, it's only ten minutes taxi drive from here, I discovered it quite by chance,' said Miles. 'It's as big as Hyde Park, bigger probably, with a huge lake. It's very unkempt compared with what we're used to but quite magnificent and peaceful and above all, cool.'

'It sounds perfect,' said Keith, 'we'd better take some water with us.' They both stood up.

'I'll get that. Shall we meet in the lobby in, say, fifteen minutes?' Miles suggested.

Keith eyed him. 'You're not going to run out on me again, are you Miles?'

Miles smiled and shook his head, 'No Chief Inspector, I'm through with running, I promise.'

Half an hour later, a taxi deposited them in an

extraordinary expanse of what felt more like countryside than the middle of the city. They found a rather rusty bench in the shade and settled down.

'Where do you want me to start?' Miles asked.

'Wherever you feel most comfortable,' Keith replied.

Miles took a deep breath. 'Then I suppose I'd better start with Marianna,' he hesitated. 'Is it true what they say in the newspapers – was she a prostitute?'

'I'm afraid so,' said Keith, 'though, like so many Eastern European girls, I'm sure not by choice. She and three other girls were tricked into coming over the England. They thought they were going into proper jobs, instead they were raped and beaten into submission and ended up in the sex trade.'

'But you've got the bastard who did it from what I see in the papers.'

'Yes,' said Keith, 'and he's been charged with your sister's murder. We've got him on DNA evidence and a partial confession, but obviously we need your testament in court as to exactly what happened on that day. I assume you were in St Ives?' Miles nodded. 'Are you ready to tell me what happened?'

'I went out with some friends to a club in London the night before. You know how it is, we got drinking and talking and suddenly I realised I'd missed the sleeper, so I stayed the night with a friend and I caught an early train the following morning, aware that I had my meeting with you at three o'clock.

Because the taxis can be a bit erratic at St Erth, I left the train at Truro and got a taxi from there.'

Keith smiled. 'So that's why nobody spotted you at St Erth or St Ives.'

'I suppose it is,' said Miles. He paused again. Keith could sense him gathering his strength to tell his story. 'I arrived at the house at about midday; it felt strange with no one there but me. I'd barely got in the door when the bell went and there, standing on the doorstep, was Marianna. She was very emotional, but she managed to tell me straight out that she was my sister.'

'She spoke English then?' Keith said.

'Yes, a little. When she first left the orphanage she'd managed to get a job in a hotel, just a cleaning job, but she picked up a few words of English. She had all the key words written down on a piece of paper, she'd copied them out of the dictionary – adoption, orphanage, that sort of thing. To start with I couldn't think what she was talking about, I thought she was some mad foreign vagrant who'd ended up by chance on our doorstep. But gradually it began to dawn on me that she was, well, on the level. She didn't tell me anything about her life, just that she had come to England to find me and had read about our family in the papers because of my father's disappearance. She knew the family had to be the one who had adopted me because she had found out all the details of my adoption from the court records in Bucharest. To start with I didn't believe her, it was such a shock, I just thought she was after money.'

'Well you would, wouldn't you,' said Keith, 'you had no reason to assume you were adopted.'

'None whatsoever,' Miles said, 'initially it was unbelievable – that my parents had lied to me all my life and that here was my sister – it was just too much to take in.'

'So why did you come to believe her?' Keith asked, fascinated.

'In the end, it wasn't difficult,' said Miles. 'She pointed out the likeness between us, and then ...' he faltered. Keith waited in silence, sensing that Miles needed time, not more questions, 'and then, she rubbed the bridge of her nose, like this.' He made the gesture. 'It's what I do when I'm nervous, put on the spot. When she did that, I just knew she was telling the truth.'

'So what happened next?' Keith asked gently.

'She went on and on,' Miles said, 'saying how we used to share a cot in the orphanage and how she'd cried when I was taken away. Being three and a half years older than me she remembered it all you see. I remember nothing. It got too much.'

Keith thought fleetingly of Felicity's theory. 'So you left her for a cooling off period while you thought about what she had told you?'

Miles met Keith's eyes. 'Yes I did, and I shall regret it for the rest of my life.'

'If you'd been in the house when Jackson arrived he would have killed you both, Miles, and that is certainly not what Marianna would have wanted. He was a violent man and looking at you I can see that you haven't a streak of violence in you. You would have tried to defend yourself and your sister I'm sure, but you would have failed. Jackson is about eight inches taller than you, and twice as wide. He is capable of rape and murder – you two wouldn't have stood a chance.'

'I left her,' Miles said brokenly. He put his head in his hands and began to weep. Keith put a hand on his shoulder and then silently handed him a handkerchief.

'So Marianna agreed to stay at the house?'

'No, no, it wasn't like that. I was so upset, I simply got up and ran down the steps from the terrace. I didn't say goodbye, I didn't say I'd be back, I didn't say anything, I just went, I couldn't cope. I can't believe I did that.'

'She must have understood,' said Keith, 'or she would have left too. She clearly waited for you in the house, believing that you would come back. If only she hadn't let Jackson in.'

'I wonder why she did,' Miles answered.

'I expect,' said Keith, thinking of no other way to put it, 'that she thought it was you returning. It wasn't until she opened the door and saw it was Jackson that she realised her mistake – by which time it was too late,' Keith hesitated, 'you did come back I presume, Miles?'

He nodded. 'I was only gone for about half an

hour. I ran down onto Porthmeor beach and marched about for a bit to try to calm myself. Then I realised how cruel and ungrateful I had been to Marianna. She had made this huge effort to find me and she wasn't to know that my parents hadn't told me I was adopted. She'd travelled all this way to find me, suffered God knows what horrors and I'd run out on her. So I literally ran back up again. When I arrived on the terrace I thought she must have gone, I was frantic. The front door was shut, so I had a moment's hope that she was still there in the house. I called her, there was no reply, so I opened the front door with my key …' his voice broke, '… and there she was.'

'It was a terrible sight,' said Keith, 'it affected me and my sergeant greatly and we had no connection with her.'

Miles ignored him. 'I knew she was dead, although I'd never seen a dead body before. I just panicked, I forgot all about the meeting with you. All I could think about was that she was dead. I couldn't think how she'd died or why she was dead. I even wondered if I was going mad and in my agitation, I had killed her. I also thought that maybe it was a hallucination.'

'So you ran away again?' said Keith.

'Yes, I don't remember what happened next. I do know I walked and walked and somehow ended up on the Hayle by-pass. A lorry driver stopped and offered me a lift, he was going to Bodmin. He dropped me at the station and I caught a train the following morning.'

'I wonder why he didn't come forward?'

'Who?' Miles asked.

'The lorry driver, we've flashed your face all over the place, as you must be aware, in an effort to find you – he must have recognised you.'

'Probably not,' said Miles, 'by the time I ended up on the by-pass it was dark. He asked me what I was doing and I said I was on holiday down in Cornwall and I needed to get back home to London. He seemed to accept my story, turned up his music and I don't think we said another word until he dropped me off at Bodmin Parkway station.'

'So when did you decide to come to Bucharest?'

'That night,' said Miles, 'while I was sitting in the station. The initial shock had worn off a bit and all I could think about was going to Bucharest and finding out who I was and, if possible, more about Marianna. Luckily, I'd left my rucksack on the terrace and amazingly had the sense to pick it up when I'd found Marianna's body. It meant I had my passport with me. Looking so young for my age means I always need ID for a night out – it's the first time I've ever been grateful for looking like a kid.'

'Believe me, you'll be glad one day that you don't look your age,' Keith said sagely. 'Tell me, do you feel you've been successful in your quest?'

'I've discovered nothing good – my birth parents are dead, I also know I have no siblings other than Marianna. We were sent to Orphanage Number 1 shortly after I was born and it was there that Marianna and I were cared for until I was adopted.' He shuddered. 'I'm told the orphanage is much better than it was when we were there. God knows, then, what it was like when it's still so terrible now. Rows of cots, rows of unwanted children half mad from lack of love, it's terrible.'

'I thought the orphanage problem in Romania was solved,' said Keith.

'That's what everyone thinks but the country is still full of abandoned children. When I am twenty-one and I come into my inheritance, that's where it's going, to improve the lot of children out here.'

'That's an excellent notion,' said Keith. He hesitated, 'Miles, I'd like you to come home with me.'

'Home,' said Miles bitterly, 'where's home?'

'Home is in London with your mother, the only mother you'll ever know. She may have lied to you but she loves you very much, I know that. You need to talk, she needs to explain herself. She was devastated by your father's disappearance but it's nothing compared with the grief she is feeling over you. I want to book us seats on the flight out to Heathrow tomorrow morning.'

'You'll find it a hard job to get seats at such short notice.'

Keith grinned. 'I have my ways.'

Miles smiled back. 'I'm sure you have Chief Inspector. I appreciate you coming out here, it's helped to be able to talk to you, to talk to someone.

It's just I can't stop thinking of Marianna's life compared with mine. Why on earth didn't they adopt us both?'

'That's probably the most important question you will need to ask your mother,' said Keith.

12

It had been agreed that Keith and Miles should meet for dinner that evening in the hotel restaurant. Miles had been clearly exhausted by his conversation with Keith; if they were to leave Bucharest in the morning he had some loose ends to tie up he told Keith.

'You'll ring your mother and tell her you're coming home, will you?' Keith asked.

'Could you?' Miles said, avoiding eye contact.

'As you wish,' said Keith.

Once back in the hotel, they had a quick restorative drink at the bar before Miles took off with great speed and purpose. It left Keith a little apprehensive – the boy had disappeared once, would he do it again?

It was a question of judgement and trust. He had presented himself to Keith as being both honest and sincere. He had promised to come home and on reflection there were really no grounds to doubt the boy's sincerity and yet … Remembering what Miles had said about money oiling the wheels of everything in Romania, Keith presented himself to the hotel reception manager, showed his warrant card, explained that Miles was in no trouble but was a young lad who needed to be kept an eye on. For a twenty pound note Keith secured round the clock surveillance on Miles to make sure he didn't check out. Keith was confident he was not the sort of boy who would leave the hotel without paying his bill.

With an afternoon to kill before meeting Miles in the restaurant Keith first arranged their flights back, rang Barbara to tell her what he was up to and then Lady Irving. She answered the telephone on the first ring which made him feel guilty for not telephoning her first.

'Have you found him?' she asked without preamble.

'Yes,' said Keith, 'he's safe and well and I'm bringing him home tomorrow.'

'You'll bring him here?' she asked.

'We haven't worked out the details yet,' said Keith, 'but I do have to get back to Cornwall.'

'I'll meet the flight if you give me the details.'

'Heathrow Terminal Two,' said Keith. 'Hang on a moment I'll give you the flight number.' With the details recorded the relief was evident in Lady Irving's voice. 'Do you want me to tell him you'll be meeting him?'

She hesitated for a moment. 'I don't want to frighten him off,' she said, 'probably better not.'

'I'll have to tell him what happens when we

'arrive at Heathrow.'

'Just tell him I've sent a car, that's what we normally do.' How the other half lives, Keith thought.

'OK,' he said, 'that's fine, if it sounds plausible to him.'

'Absolutely,' said Lady Irving, she hesitated. 'I am most grateful Chief Inspector, I know you don't approve of certain aspects of how we've brought up our son, but I do love him very much and after the terrible shock that he has endured, I will do everything in my power to make things right for him.'

'I'm sure you will,' said Keith, soothingly.

After the phone calls and he had completed his paperwork, it was still early afternoon, Keith was at a loss as to what to do next. Almost for something better to do, he raided the hotel mini-bar and poured himself a whisky and water, then he stood by the window staring out at what he now knew was Parliament Square. The sun still blazed but somehow it couldn't warm the stone of the buildings around him. Despite the heat and colour of the sun, the buildings remained as drab as they would do on a cold February morning. He thought about the affect of light on stone; how sunlight warmed the great buildings in London – St Paul's Cathedral, Westminster Abbey, the wonderful buildings along the Mall leading to Buckingham Palace. He thought of Oxford, a city he had come to know better now since meeting Felicity Paradise and the way the sun brought the old colleges to life, giving the stone a depth and hue. Even Truro Cathedral, sometimes criticised as a piece of Victorian melodrama, came to life when the sun shone ... but not Bucharest. Decision made, he drained his glass and went downstairs to the hotel reception once more. His request was for a taxi driver who spoke a little English and within moments he found himself in the back of a battered-looking Mercedes.

'Where do you want to go?' asked the taxi driver in a strong American accent. The sight of him was rather an alarming experience, for the man had a huge black moustache and a set of brilliant white teeth. 'I guess the American accent confuses you,' he said, 'I worked in Texas for a couple of years, my cousin has a restaurant there. So where to?'

'I don't know,' said Keith, 'just drive me around Bucharest for quarter of an hour, half an hour, whatever you think it takes to show me the sights.'

They talked as they drove. The taxi driver pointing out drab building after drab building – the new television centre, the new hospital.

'What bought you back?' Keith asked.

'I left Romania as soon as we were able to travel, I needed to put some space between me and all the misery.'

'I don't understand,' Keith said.

'While Ceausescu was alive, we were prisoners in our own country – none of us had passports, we could go nowhere.'

'I hadn't realised,' said Keith.

'Not many people do outside Romania. By 1991 however, we could go anywhere and an awful lot of us left.'

'But you came back.'

'I came back because I expected it to be better.'

'And is it?' Keith asked.

The taxi driver's shoulders rose and fell in a large sigh. 'No, worse. It's safer but the Securitate, the Secret Police, have just been replaced by the Mafia. Goods are now available in the shops in a way they never were before but no one can afford them. It just breeds envy. Before the revolution we did not know what we were missing.'

They were driving down a wide street, rather reminiscent of the Mall. Ahead of them two enormous buildings loomed white in contrast to the grey around them.

'What on earth are they?' Keith asked.

'The his and hers palaces, Ceausescu had them built for him and his wife. They bulldozed thousands of homes in order to create this space in the middle of the city.' He stopped the car close to the gates of the larger of the two palaces. 'My parents' house was one of them, no compensation, nothing, one day they had a home, the next they didn't.'

'Terrible,' said Keith, 'these are ...' he searched for words.

'Obscene,' the taxi driver suggested.

'That'll do,' said Keith. The car was sweltering, there was no air conditioning. 'I'd like to get out for a moment, if I may,' said Keith.

'Go ahead, I'll join you.'

The two men leant against the car and stared up at the buildings. 'Do you know much about the orphanages?' Keith asked.

'I was involved during the time so many western couples came over to adopt. I had a little English even then, and German, I'm good at languages.'

'You certainly are,' said Keith.

'I took couples to orphanages, helped them collect babies, go to the passport office, go to the court. It was a grateful American couple who helped me get my visa.'

'You sound as if you don't approve?'

'No,' the huge moustache bristled with denial. 'No it's not disapproval, it just didn't solve the problem.'

'How do you mean?' Keith asked.

'I don't know the number of adoptions – a few thousand children, started a new life, had hope, a future but tens of thousands of children stayed where they were rotting in those places. The orphanages are bad enough in Bucharest, they're terrible in the country districts.'

'Still?' Keith asked.

'Oh yes, as I said, nothing really changes here in Romania. On the surface yes, the shops are full and we're soon to join the EU – but ask the peasant farmer, the five year old child alone and mad, rocking in his orphanage cot, ask the factory worker, ask the exhausted woman, pregnant with her sixth child who still cannot get contraception even though it's supposed to be available – nothing has changed for them ...' he hesitated and turned to Keith, 'or me.'

The encounter left Keith uncharacteristically depressed. As essentially a man of action, reflection was not a natural state for him in. He showered and changed and presented himself at the bar at six o'clock. He and Miles were due to meet at six-thirty. As the minutes ticked by and well into his second whisky, Keith grew increasingly apprehensive but on the dot of half past six Miles entered the bar. Keith was weak with relief. The boy ordered a lager and without preamble they agreed on an early dinner. Once seated and their meal ordered, Keith studied Miles, he seemed less agitated than he had in the morning, altogether calmer.

'What have you done with your day?' Miles asked.

Keith told him. 'I spoke to your mother. She is sending a car to the airport.' Miles nodded without comment. 'And I had a tour of Bucharest, compliments of a particularly informative taxi driver.'

'What did you think?' Miles asked.

'I thought it was terrible,' Keith replied. 'There are some fine old buildings but there is such an air of depression about the place. I went to the palaces.'

'Oh, did you, hideous aren't they?' said Miles.

Keith nodded. 'I talked to the taxi driver about the orphanages too,' he said, 'I gather not much has changed there.'

Miles shook his head. 'That's where I've been this afternoon. I went to Orphanage Number 1. I've been before and the staff there have been very kind so I went to thank them and take them a present.'

'What did you take them?' Keith asked curiously.

Miles managed one of his rare smiles. 'A coffee percolator,' he said, 'and an almost unlimited supply of coffee, it's what they wanted more than anything.'

'That sounds an excellent present,' said Keith. He hesitated, wondering if he was intruding on too many raw emotions. 'Is it hard to leave or will you be relieved to get back to England?'

Miles considered the question. He took so long to answer that Keith wondered whether he was going to answer at all and was starting to regret the question. 'A bit of both, I suppose,' he said at last, 'I don't feel I belong here anymore. Maybe it would be different if I could find my birth family but since none of them are alive ...' his voice trailed away and into the silence Keith's mobile phone began to ring. He answered it quickly, apologising. He was half out of his chair to leave the restaurant in order to take the call, when the news he heard was so stunning he sat back in his seat.

'Are you sure, absolutely sure, only I'm with Miles Irving now, as you know?'

Miles looked up at the mention of his name. The

policeman had gone very pale. Something was up, he felt his heart thudding in his chest. He didn't think he could cope with any more dramas. Keith thanked the caller and returned the mobile phone to his pocket, then he looked up and met Miles' seye. He's a nice man, Miles thought, fleetingly. He's going to tell me something shocking and he's worried sick about how I'll feel.

'That was my superintendent,' Keith said, 'you need to prepare yourself for another shock to the system, I'm afraid, Miles, a good one this time though.'

'What?' Miles asked.

'It's your father, he's turned up at home in Notting Hill, about two hours ago apparently.'

It was Miles's turn to look more than a little pale. 'Are you sure?'

'Yes,' said Keith, 'that's the first question I asked. I didn't want there to be any slip up, any mistake – you've had enough adjustments to make in the last couple of weeks. It is definitely him and he is definitely at home with your mother now. He suffered from amnesia apparently. He remembers going into the water, he remembers taking a wave and then everything is a blank. Then about a week ago he started to remember things. He was in Jersey working as barman in a hotel.'

'A what,' said Miles, 'are you sure? The whole thing sounds incredibly implausible.' Keith privately agreed with him. 'So he just eventually remembered who he was, got on a plane back from Jersey and turned up at home?'

'That's how it would appear to be,' said Keith, 'obviously, once we get back, you'll know more.'

'Somebody would have recognised him on Jersey, surely and how did he get there, he'd have needed a passport. Your certainly don't carry a passport on you when you're surfing.'

'I don't know, Miles, I don't know any more than you do,' said Keith. 'I do know that amnesia is a genuine condition. We had a case in Truro not so long ago – a man walked out of the family home one day and couldn't remember his way back for three years.'

Miles shook his head. 'I just don't know what to think,' he said.

'If I may say so,' said Keith, 'you don't seem overjoyed by the news.'

'I don't like him,' said Miles, 'that's the truth of it. I never have liked him very much and now I know he's not my father, it is easier to face how I feel!'

The flight back to Heathrow was uneventful and touched down on time. As they left the baggage hall and headed for Arrivals, Keith wondered what on earth was going through Miles's mind. He was apparently calm and composed, but then Keith imagined he was still assuming that there would simply be a car to meet him. Keith on the other hand rather expected there would be a reception committee, and indeed there was – not just Sir Hugo and Lady Irving but a bevy of reporters.

'Oh God,' said Miles, when he saw the sight.

'I'll catch you in a day or two,' said Keith, 'I've got most of your statement together – we can compare notes on it and you can sign it up in London. We'll need to talk about Marianna too – you'll want a funeral, of course.' They were standing together in the entrance of Arrivals, the press were pushing forward; Sir Hugo, standing beside his wife, looked well and tanned. Was it all just some crazy publicity stunt, Keith wondered. He felt bad about bringing the boy back to this, handing him over to the press for a feeding frenzy. 'Can you cope?' he asked.

'Oh yes,' said Miles, 'I'm used to this.' He smiled at Keith. 'Thanks, thanks for everything, let me know as soon as you can release my sister.' Squaring his shoulders he headed towards his parents. His mother swept him into an embrace, the cameras flashed. For some reason Keith couldn't quite identify, the whole spectacle made him feel uneasy. While the focus was on the Irving family, Keith slipped away and headed towards the car park.

At Exeter services he stopped for a coffee and noticed for the first time that he had seven missed calls, one of which was from Felicity Paradise. She answered her phone immediately.

'Goodness,' she said, without preamble, 'when

you decide to solve a case you really go for it, Chief Inspector, don't you?'

Keith laughed. 'Well it does seem I'm somewhat redundant so far as the Irvings are concerned, thank God.'

'What do you make of Sir Hugo turning up like that?' Felicity asked.

'I don't know,' said Keith, 'I have none of the details at the moment, other than he has apparently been suffering from amnesia and came to in Jersey.'

'Do you believe it?'

'I don't know that either,' said Keith, 'but as his son said, it all sounds rather implausible. I think Miles has always seen Hugo as very controlling. He can't grasp the idea of Hugo not being in control – for losing the plot completely, like that. It's out of character.'

'How is Miles?'

'OK – he is an odd combination really, quite vulnerable, well very vulnerable in many respects, but also resilient. He coped brilliantly at the airport. There were press and all sorts, as you can imagine, plus two parents he hadn't seen since Marianna told him of his adoption.'

'So what happens now?' Felicity asked.

'Well,' said Keith, 'case closed I suppose. I have a mass of paperwork to complete of course. We have to make absolutely sure that the case against Jackson sticks, but it should do, no reason why not. The Irvings clearly have a lot of work to do if they are to rebuild themselves as a family but that's hardly a police matter. It's extraordinary really, forty-eight hours ago, I had two missing people and the world's press howling at me and now it's all over.'

'You sound almost regretful,' said Felicity.

'Believe me,' said Keith, 'I'm absolutely not, I'm relieved as hell. Us Cornish coppers are not used to all this publicity – it was all a bit high profile for me.'

Felicity laughed. 'The Irving house in St Ives is up for sale,' she said.

'Oh really?'

'It's hardly surprising, is it?' said Felicity, 'I'm sure Miles will never want to go there again, though whether they'll find a buyer with such a hideous murder having taken place so recently, I don't know.'

'There's some odd people out there,' said Keith, 'they might even like the notoriety.'

'Maybe,' said Felicity, doubtfully. 'So you'll have a weekend off now, will you?'

'Good Lord, it's Friday isn't it, yes I suppose I will, though I just want to arrange for Marianna's body to be released for burial. I think Miles needs that.'

'Poor boy,' said Felicity, 'it was clever of you to realise that he would go to Romania. It is an obvious move, I don't know why it never occurred to me.'

'I can take absolutely no credit for that,' said Keith, 'Barbara came up with the idea, though had the grace of adding that as a mere male, I couldn't have been expected to work it out.' The memory of

Barbara's rather derogatory comments about Felicity flashed into his mind. 'Anyway,' he said firmly, 'I am most grateful for all your help.'

'My pleasure Chief Inspector.'

Felicity put down her mobile and stared out across St Ives Bay. She was sitting on the balcony of Jericho Cottage, enjoying the afternoon sunshine. She barely knew Sir Hugo Irving, she had never met Miles and had only seen Lady Irving at a distance. She had no intimate knowledge of the family at all and yet something niggled at the edge of her mind telling her that something was wrong, it was all too easy and that Keith Penrose's case was very far from closed. He was a good policeman and a very decent human being, but she felt that the Irving case had him way out of his depth, which in turn was clouding his judgement. The high profile nature of the Irving family, the intense media interest and the fact that Keith had even found himself in the limelight, had all made him extremely uncomfortable. He just wanted to close the file, but in doing so was closing his mind to the idea that something was still not right. Felicity was sure – it wasn't over yet.

13

Sunday morning dawned a bright and blustery day. Felicity had promised herself a few hours off. Jamie and his family were due in two weeks time and she only had two plants still to paint to complete her assignment. If she worked hard she reckoned she should have it all wrapped up by the time her family arrived. She found herself to be very tired, having painted relentlessly for days. She had a long hot bath, washed her hair and had breakfast on the balcony in her dressing gown feeling very decadent. It was after eleven before she was dressed and ready to face the day.

She was still washing up her breakfast things when the doorbell rang. Felicity looked up surprised, she was not used to visitors on a Sunday. Sunday was a family day and her family was far away. She went downstairs and opened her front door to find her daughter Mel and her old friend Martin Tregonning standing together on the doorstep. Mel looked radiant and sun-tanned, Martin looked good too, bronzed and fit from an outdoor life running his garden centre in

Hayle. She hugged them both. Martin, she noticed, was carrying a bottle of champagne – could that possibly mean … she didn't dare hope.

'Come up,' she said, 'this is an unexpected pleasure.'

'We have something to tell you, Mum,' said Mel, 'and then we're going to take you out to lunch, that's assuming you're free, knowing you and your hectic social life.'

'I'm completely free,' said Felicity, leading the way into the kitchen, 'in fact, I have to admit I've only just got up. What have you to tell me, something good, I hope?'

They sat round the kitchen table and Mel took Felicity's hand.

'It is slightly the wrong way round, Mum, but I'm going to have a baby and Martin and I have decided to get married.'

Felicity looked from one to the other. 'Are you sure?'

They both looked crestfallen. 'Aren't you pleased?' Mel asked.

'I'm absolutely thrilled but I've waited so long for this moment, I just can't believe it's actually happening.'

Martin smiled. 'It's my fault, the time it's taken. I have been so frightened of a commitment after what happened to Helen, yet I've known right from the beginning that Mel was the one – if she'd have me, that is.'

Felicity pulled herself together. 'I am so pleased for you both,' she said and standing up kissed them each in turn, 'so what happens now?'

'We open the champagne,' said Martin.

Felicity laughed. 'You know perfectly well what I mean.'

'We thought just a small affair in St Ives church and then maybe we could take over one of the restaurants for lunch, nothing posh and not a lot of people – just a few friends and family.'

'And a baby, you are clever and how exciting! How are you feeling Mel?'

'Sick, most of the time,' Mel admitted.

'And what about your job and where will you live?' asked Felicity.

'My firm have been threatening to open a branch in Truro for some time and it looks like they might actually do it – they've found a property at last. By the time I've finished my maternity leave, with any luck they might even have got their act together.'

'That would be marvellous,' said Felicity, 'and where will you live?'

'Well, as you know, Martin has sunk all his money into the business and he only rents in Hayle but he is making money at last so he has some income.'

'Of sorts,' said Martin.

'So between us we should be able to get a mortgage. We'd like to live in St Ives but prices are so high, it'll probably be Hayle.'

'Darling, you living in Hayle,' Felicity said, 'that's just the most wonderful news.'

'Carefully chosen so that Granny can babysit,' Martin said, and they all laughed. The champagne was poured.

'Just give me half a glass,' said Mel, 'and then while you two get stuck into the bottle, I'll whip down and see Annie and tell her the news.'

Ever since Mel had resigned from her job in London two years before, come home miserable and confused and still mourning her father, she and Annie had formed a close bond. Annie was like that, Felicity thought, as she watched her daughter rushing down the stairs. She too had been scooped up by Annie's loving care and sheltered under her protective wing during the worst period of her life.

With Mel gone Martin refilled their glasses.

'Shall we go and sit on the balcony,' said Felicity. He nodded. 'Pity to miss the sunshine, it's a lovely day.'

Comfortably seated and before Felicity could say a word, Martin raised his glass. 'To my future mother-in-law,' he said. 'Are you really happy with this, Felicity, I know I'm a lot older than Mel, but I'll take great care of her, I really will.'

'I know you will,' said Felicity, 'I've been hoping for such a long time that you two would get together, and I do understand how hard it must have been for you to dare make a serious commitment again.'

Martin's wife, Helen, pregnant with their first child, had been killed in a car accident three years previously. When Felicity had first met Martin, quite by chance on the pier in St Ives shortly after her arrival in the town, they had both been recently bereaved and as a result a strong bond had formed between them. To have such a good friend join the family was a very cosy feeling and she said so.

'I'm glad you feel like that,' he said. 'I have to admit, I was worried about how you would react to the news.'

'Well you didn't need to be worried,' said Felicity, 'though you do realise, don't you, that you're taking on quite a handful – she's an awfully strong-minded girl.'

'Don't I know it,' said Martin, 'but I do think we're pretty well suited – I'm fairly bumbly and chaotic and Mel's so organised and decisive. I don't think Mel could stand it if she had a partner who was competing to be in charge, and I don't think I can cope long-term without somebody like Mel in my life to organise me. It's perfect!'

Felicity laughed, 'I think you're probably right, Martin.'

'I'm nervous of course,' Martin said, after a moment, 'terribly frightened for Mel in case anything should happen to her and the baby.'

'That expression, "lightning never strikes twice", is probably an appropriate one for you to focus on,'

Felicity said. 'Mel's going to be fine and so is your baby and from what you've told me of Helen, she would be pleased to know you are happy and settled at last.'

'Yes, she would,' said Martin. 'She wouldn't have wanted me moping about on my own, she had such a generous nature. Comparisons are odious – Mel is a much stronger character than Helen but she has a gentle side too.'

Felicity looked incredulous – she loved her daughter dearly but 'Mel' and 'gentle' were not two words she could ever imagine in the same sentence. Seeing her expression, Martin smiled, 'Truly she does – for example, it's rather touching, Mel suggested the other day that if the baby is a girl we should call her Helen.' Felicity was touched, Mel must really love this man she thought.

'Anyway,' Martin said, 'that's enough about us, what about you? It's about time we found you someone special. I take it there isn't anyone at the moment?'

Felicity shook her head. 'No, nor likely to be.'

'You can't say that, not at fifty,' Martin protested.

Felicity sighed and smiled at him sadly. 'There are very few available single men in my sort of age group but even if there were a plentiful supply, a terrible weariness overcomes me every time I think about the concept of a new relationship. Charlie and I had our ups and downs, particularly towards the end, but we understood each other. We'd been together since we were very young and a lot of what we did and said happened by osmosis. We were two halves of a whole. I will never achieve that with anyone else, nor share their children.'

'No, of course it wouldn't be the same,' Martin interrupted, 'but there's no reason why it shouldn't be equally fulfilling – just in a different sort of way.'

'And then,' said Felicity, 'if it won't embarrass you to mention it, there's the whole sex thing. When you've lived with somebody since you were young, you can both remember when you were half-decent to look at, with or without clothes. However, all the sags and wrinkles would be acutely embarrassing, if they were to be shared with someone who hadn't known you for years. Honestly, I couldn't do it, Martin.'

'All I can say is that looking at the problem from where I'm sitting,' said Martin, 'you look pretty damn trim to me, Mrs Paradise.'

'I think it is probably illegal to flirt with your future mother-in-law,' Felicity said sternly.

At that moment the front door banged downstairs and Mel erupted onto the balcony followed by Annie, who hugged and kissed everyone.

'Didn't I tell you, Felicity, that these two were made for each other,' she said.

'You did indeed.'

'Well there you go then, old Annie does get it right sometimes.'

'Old Annie gets in right always,' said Martin.

'Creep,' mother and daughter chorused.

Later that evening, alone again, Felicity mulled over the day's events. She was completely happy about the pending marriage of Mel and Martin. Annie was right, they were made for each other, they brought out the best in one another, complimented each other and there was every chance they would be very happy together. So that meant both her children were settled, and now there was another grandchild on the way.

Fleetingly into her mind came the thought of Keith Penrose's Carly, in remission now, bravely carving a new career, but with the spectre of the disease still hanging over her, and the knowledge that chemotherapy had probably robbed her of the chance of motherhood.

I'm so lucky, Felicity thought, then why the sense of melancholy? Was it because suddenly she was peripheral? It was a long time since she had been the centre of her children's world, but while Mel was single, Felicity had felt that she and Mel were still a family unit. Now, of course, Mel and Martin would be a family and Felicity would be spare, a granny, but an outsider to the immediate family circle.

She thought back over her conversation with Martin. It was true, she didn't feel up to a new and intimate relationship with anyone and yet the reality was that at fifty, she could live for another thirty years – thirty years alone. She stood up as if to shake herself free of her thoughts and put on the kettle. Look at Annie, she had been widowed for years and her life was completely fulfilled. Surely it was possible to achieve the same peace of mind.

'Why did you have to die, Charlie?' she said out loud. The shock of finding out about Charlie's past, and of the secrets he had kept from her, was starting to fade. Increasingly these days she just missed him, missed being married to him, being with him; she ached for him. It was all such a waste.

While Felicity was mourning her lost marriage, Jack and Maggie Curnow had just celebrated theirs in the time-honoured way. Maggie was lying comfortably in the crook of Jack's arm.

'I'm sorry, Jack,' she said, 'I know I've given you a really hard time recently but it won't happen no more. I have got to accept your way of life and learn to put up with it.'

'Blimey,' said Jack, 'what bought that on?'

'Your boss came to see me, didn't you know?' Jack shook his head. 'He explained a few things to me, one of them was that I should be proud of what you do and he is right Jack, I should be. It was you who found Miles Irving, wasn't it?'

'Sort of,' Jack agreed.

'Well, there you go,' said Maggie, 'you're doing something important, something worthwhile and all I've been doing is criticising you for being late for supper.'

Jack twisted in the bed so he could have a better look at his wife. 'Do you really mean all this, love?'

'I really do,' she said.

'That's just great, I've been so miserable, I hate us falling out all the time.'

'There's going to be some changes,' said Maggie, 'I'm going to make my own life, for me and the baby, and sometimes you'll have to fit in with us, not me always hanging around for you.'

'That's as it should be,' said Jack.

'It's what the Chief Inspector said,' Maggie confirmed. 'He's a nice man, your boss, Jack.'

'That's not what you normally say, you usually don't have a good word to say for him.'

'I know, but that was the old me. I'm not saying I'll never grumble again but I realise that what you two get up to is important and I'm going to try and remember that.' They kissed and snuggled close.

'Thanks, boss,' Jack thought.

Keith Penrose couldn't sleep and got up early on Sunday morning to walk the dog. On the way back to the house he collected the Sunday papers which were still full of the Irvings. Barbara was in the kitchen brewing some coffee.

'I've been thinking,' said Keith, 'instead of you slaving over a hot stove, let's go out to lunch.'

'But I've got the joint,' said Barbara.

'It'll keep. Why don't we go to the Ferry Boat Inn?'

'It'll be very crowded this time of year.'

'It will,' said Keith, 'but if we go early, we'll be able to get a table.'

'What about Carly, she'll expect her Sunday lunch?'

'Leave Carly to me,' said Keith.

Keith knocked on his daughter's bedroom door. She was sitting up in bed surrounded by textbooks; she had exams the following week.

'Hi Dad,' she patted the bed, 'how are you doing? Case all wrapped up I understand,' she smiled at him, 'well done, clever old thing.'

'Less of the old,' said Keith, 'I was thinking of taking your mother out to lunch today, to the Ferry Boat at Helford Passage, I thought.'

'Goodness, that's a first,' said Carly, 'what's bought this on?'

Keith shrugged. 'I don't know, just thought it might be a nice gesture. Do you want to come?'

'Actually, no,' said Carly, 'if that's alright. To be honest, it's quite a relief to be let off the Sunday lunch routine, for once. I can meet some chums in town instead, do a few pubs.'

'Don't drink too much,' said Keith, 'you need to look after yourself.'

'Dad,' Carly warned, 'don't start.'

'Sorry,' he stood up and leant over, kissing the top of her head, 'have fun, darling.'

'And you,' she called as he closed the door behind him.

They reached the Ferry Boat shortly before midday and had no trouble securing a table on the terrace. Keith ordered some food, and a bottle of wine and joined his wife. It was a beautiful, typically English summer's day. Small children were making sandcastles on the beach below them, some slightly older children were launching a rubber dinghy. The ferry was going backwards and forwards between the inn and the Shipwright's on the other side of the Helford River. Yachts were coming and going, tenders were flashing between them and the shore – it was busy yes, but in a relaxed and tranquil way.

'This is nice, Keith,' Barbara conceded, 'and I like the menu here.' This was praise indeed from Barbara for whom food was very important.

'We should do it more often,' said Keith.

'We'll be able to when you retire,' said Barbara. Keith looked immediately uncomfortable. 'You're not looking forward to retirement, are you?' said Barbara.

It was a difficult question to answer without upsetting her.

'I suppose I'm not really,' he admitted, cautiously. 'I've been a policeman for so long I don't know what happens when I stop being one. I wonder whether there is anybody else still there. Do you understand what I mean?'

'Yes,' said Barbara, 'I do. I think it will be tough for you to start with but I wouldn't be surprised if you don't end up rather enjoying it.'

'Maybe,' Keith said, 'certainly this Irving case has made me feel ...' he shook his head, 'I don't know how to explain.'

'Was it the body of the girl which upset you so much?' Barbara asked.

'Yes, that and the life she had been forced to lead ... and what I saw of Romania depressed me. We are so lucky living on this funny little island of ours. Romania is a beautiful country, so I understand, but rather like the Balkans, it's in the wrong place – for centuries people just moved in, conquered it, exploited it and then moved on. I mean look at this place,' he gestured to the Helford River laid out before them, 'it's so beautiful and it's on our doorstep. What a privilege it is to be British, to be Cornish.' His expression suddenly softened.

And no one will ever move me from this land,
Until the Lord calls me to sit at his hand.
For this is my Eden, and I'm not alone,
For this is my Cornwall and this is my home.

'You soft git, Keith,' Barbara said, when he finished, though she was clearly moved, 'you're not suited to being a policeman really.'

'Bit late now,' said Keith, smiling at her.

'So what will happen to Sir Hugo Irving?' Barbara asked, obviously trying to lighten the mood.

Keith shrugged. 'It's not a crime to get hit over

172

the head by a surfboard, forget who you are, then remember and go home.'

'Provided, of course, that everybody's satisfied with the explanation.'

'Either way, Hugo is home and Miles is home, though, of course, the family will never be the same again. There is certainly no love lost between Miles and his father and then there is poor Marianna – it will take some time for all concerned to learn to live with her death.'

At that moment their food arrived and when the waitress had gone Keith smiled at Barbara. 'Enough of the Irvings,' he said, 'they may have done their disappearing act on my patch but they're home in London now – not my patch, not my problem and that's an end to it.'

14

There were five days to go until the August bank holiday weekend, after which Jamie and his family would be arriving. There had been several wet days but at last Felicity had been able to get over to the Mount. The young girl, Sarah Cunningham, who had been so helpful on Tresco, was now back doing work experience on the Mount and had proved to be a great help, not only in finding plant specimens but also arranging times and places for Felicity to paint in peace, even sometimes when the gardens were not open to the public. It was with some considerable regret that, on her final day of painting, Felicity wiped her brushes for the last time, recognising that what work remained to be done could be tackled at home.

It was the Wednesday evening before the bank holiday, she was two days ahead of her self-imposed deadline. As she reached the harbour, she saw that several boats were arriving containing what were clearly special visitors – everyone was formally dressed. She saw Sarah ahead of her by a Land Rover, helping an elderly lady climb aboard. Everyone else was picking their way over the cobbles heading up towards the castle.

'What's going on?' Felicity asked, as she joined Sarah.

'There's a concert up at the Chapel tonight in aid of some charity. I offered to hang on to make sure everyone could get up there alright – it's quite a climb if you're not fit, as you know.'

'How do they get back?' Felicity asked.

'The tide will be out by the time the concert is over so everybody can walk back across the causeway and there will be the Land Rover on hand as well.'

'It's a very special place this, isn't it?' Felicity said.

Sarah nodded. 'I'm going to miss it terribly. It's alright for you, you can come back and paint here anytime but I'll be stuck back in college.'

'Yes, but being commissioned to do these illustrations has given a purpose to it all. I think I'll find it difficult to come back and paint without a goal.

They watched as the concertgoers streamed past them. The men were all in suits, the women smartly dressed except when it came to their feet – everyone had more sense than to try and totter around in high heels.

'Good Lord,' said Felicity suddenly, 'there are the Irvings.'

'The who?' Sarah asked.

'The Irvings,' Felicity whispered, 'Sir Hugo and Lady Irving, you know, the chap who disappeared. I don't want them to think we're staring.' Felicity turned away as the Irvings walked past her. Turning back she saw Bettine stumble slightly and Sir Hugo put a protective arm around her, helping her over the cobbles. 'I heard they were staying at the Tregenna Castle Hotel,' Felicity said, 'their house is up for sale, not surprisingly, after the murder.'

'What murder?' Sarah asked.

'Where on earth have you been? It's been all over the papers for weeks.'

'Tresco,' said Sarah with a laugh. 'I never have time to read the papers when I'm there, nor any inclination to do so, but I can see why you asked me about Bob Barnes. It was Sir Hugo you were thinking about, wasn't it, when you said you had a missing friend?' Felicity nodded. 'He does look very like Bob cleaned up and with a haircut. Funny that really – first Sir Hugo disappears and then Bob. Come on, if you want a lift back on one of the boats, you need to be quick.'

'What?' said Felicity. 'What did you say?'

'I was just saying what a coincidence it is. Come on, quick, or you really will miss the boat.

'Hang on a minute,' said Felicity, 'what's a coincidence?'

'That Bob disappeared too – he left Tresco all of a sudden and nobody knows where he's gone.'

'You never told me,' Felicity said accusingly.

'Didn't I? Oh, sorry,' said Sarah, 'though I can't see it's relevant to anything.'

'It could be,' said Felicity. 'When did Bob leave?

'Look, are you going to catch a boat or not?' Sarah said.

'Not,' said Felicity, 'I need to hear about this.'

'You'll be stuck on the Mount for the next four hours, if you don't go now. It's the last trip over tonight, you realise that?'

'That's OK,' said Felicity, 'I'm not in a hurry, I just need to hear all about Bob's disappearance.'

'This is ridiculous,' said Sarah. 'Look, I'll come with you – if we go to the mainland together, we can talk there and have a drink at the Godolphin Arms, otherwise you're going to be stranded here for hours with nothing to do but wait for the tide.'

'OK,' Felicity said. 'I'll buy supper if you like.'

'Now that's an offer I can't refuse,' said Sarah. 'Come on then, quick, the boatmen are getting restless.'

In Marazion they bought drinks and settled down at a corner table on the terrace of the Godolphin Arms, looking out over the Mount. It was a busy night, noisy, people everywhere.

'It would have been better if we'd stayed on the Mount to talk,' Felicity grumbled. 'This is really important, Sarah, when exactly did Bob disappear?'

'I knew you'd ask me that and I was trying to remember on the boat as we were coming over. It must have been two weeks ago – he went off duty on the Friday night and that was it.'

'And then you say he disappeared?'

'Just that,' said Sarah, 'the estate paid him weekly in cash, apparently, because he didn't approve of banks and bank accounts. He collected his wages on Friday and just vanished without leaving a message with anyone.'

'When did he actually leave Tresco?'

'No one knows,' said Sarah.

'So presumably, he didn't leave by helicopter or there would be a record of it?

'No, he didn't get a helicopter; I doubt he would have been able to afford it in any event. He could have taken a boat to St Mary's and then simply walked onto the Scillonian, or got a lift on a private yacht as a deckhand maybe. There's any number of ways he could have left Scilly at this time of year.'

'Have the Estate reported him missing?

'No, I shouldn't think so,' said Sarah, 'they're used to his eccentric ways. He is an odd chap, keeps himself to himself and is very independent and self-sufficient. He's disappeared before, apparently. He probably decided to go off on holiday and didn't consider it necessary to tell anyone. He'll be back in a week or two, I expect. There's no suggestion he's gone forever, his stuff is still in his cottage.'

'So if Bob disappeared just over two weeks ago and Sir Hugo reappeared ten days ago, it really is possible that they are one in the same person,' said Felicity, slowly.

'Surely not,' said Sarah.

'Well perhaps not,' Felicity agreed, 'but it's

definitely a possibility.'

'But you can't be suggesting that Sir Hugo disappeared and became Bob? Bob has been on Tresco for years.'

'I agree,' Felicity said, 'and there's the question of the infamous ponytail; there's no way Sir Hugo could have grown that, not in the time.'

'So,' said Sarah, 'it's not a question of Sir Hugo turning into Bob, it's more a question of Bob turning into Sir Hugo, is that what you're saying?'

'I rather think it is,' said Felicity, 'if you'll excuse me, I'll make a quick phone call.

Keith was still at his desk. He was ineffectually pushing pieces of paper around in order to avoid going home. The following day Carly was going to Derriford Hospital for her monthly check up and he just could not stand the tension at home. When his mobile rang he was mightily relieved – perhaps there was something he needed to do so he could avoid going home until later.

'I have a mystery for you,' Felicity said, without preamble.

Keith groaned theatrically. 'Go on,' he said.

'You remember the look-a-like on Tresco, the Sir Hugo Irving look-a-like I mean?'

'He of the straggly ponytail?'

'That's the one,' said Felicity.

'What about him?' Keith asked.

'He's disappeared.'

'What are you saying exactly?' Keith asked, serious suddenly. She had all his attention now

'I've just been talking to Sarah, Sarah Cunningham. I think I mentioned her to you – she's been doing work experience on both Tresco and here on the Mount. I was just leaving the Mount this evening when I spotted Sir Hugo and Lady Irving arriving for a concert in the chapel. I pointed them out to Sarah and that's when she told me that Bob had disappeared from Tresco about a week before Sir Hugo turned up at the family home. Do you see what I am saying?'

'Presumably that they are the same person?'

'Exactly.'

'But we've been through all this,' said Keith, 'Hugo couldn't have been Bob. Bob had been on Tresco for years and then there's that ponytail.'

'I know, I know,' said Felicity, impatiently, 'I'm not suggesting that Sir Hugo became Bob, I'm suggesting that Bob has become Sir Hugo, that he is an impostor.'

'Oh come on,' said Keith, 'you know I am always very susceptible to your more extreme ideas but this really is a bridge too far. Lady Irving and even Miles, come to that, would know immediately if the man who'd come back wasn't really Sir Hugo.'

'Yes, I suppose so,' said Felicity.

'There's no suppose about it,' said Keith, 'no one could pull off a stunt like that.'

'And another odd thing,' said Felicity undeterred, 'when they were walking past us, Lady Irving stumbled and Sir Hugo put a protective arm around her, very kindly and gently, and helped her over the cobbles.'

'So?' said Keith.

'Well that's just not a Sir Hugo-like gesture. As you know, he was always one for striding ahead, pressing flesh, calling out greetings to everyone, always the centre of attention. He would barely have noticed if his wife had tripped unless she had done herself some serious damage. The gesture was so out of character – it struck me so at the time, and I didn't even know about Bob then.'

'This is madness,' Keith said.

'OK,' said Felicity, 'I hear what you say, but you must admit it is odd that Sir Hugo's look-alike should completely disappear within a few days of his own miraculous reappearance. I think you should come over and interview him.'

'What now?'

'Yes, the concert will be over in a couple of hours.'

'I can't,' Keith said simply, 'I can't start barging into some charity concert, making accusations which are totally unfounded. Besides, which, my superintendent is there, can you imagine – mine would be the shortest serving promotion in history if I spoilt his evening by gate-crashing a get-together of the great and the good and began hurling totally unfounded accusations about. I'm sorry; I can't do anything about this.'

'You're wrong,' said Felicity.

'Alright,' said Keith, 'I am happy to accept that, just prove it.'

Keith Penrose really was the most stubborn man at times, Felicity thought as she drove out of Ludgvan, up the dark narrow lanes towards St Ives and home. It was obvious, even to a child, that the coincidence was too great. Here were two men who looked so creepily alike and one disappears as the other reappears. It was bizarre and yet Keith was refusing even to consider the possibility that she might be right. All her instincts were screaming that something was wrong but how to prove it. That's what he'd said – 'prove it'. Unusually, she felt a sudden irritation at Keith's reaction – it wasn't her job to prove anything, it was his. She was only trying to help. Clearly it would be far more convenient for him to believe the case was closed.

From the moment Felicity had heard that Sir Hugo was back she had known something wasn't right and now … it wasn't just the fact of Bob's disappearance coinciding with Hugo's reappearance that triggered her concern, it was the gesture, that solicitous, kindly gesture of Sir Hugo towards his wife as she stumbled over the cobbles. There was nothing special about that, it was the way a husband should behave towards his wife, the way anyone should behave to someone momentarily caught off balance, but it was his kindness, his concern, it was all wrong and she could not get it out of her mind.

By the time she reached Barnoon Car Park in St Ives, her thoughts were becoming increasingly confused. Maybe it was not Sir Hugo's behaviour that was flawed, maybe it was her own thinking. After all, Sir Hugo had just put his wife through the most appalling ordeal, believing for four months that he was dead. If that wasn't bad enough, they were having to cope with their extremely traumatised son who presumably was angry and resentful with them for lying about his past and denying him the opportunity of knowing his sister. Then there was Marianna's awful death which Miles must blame his parents for and which had taken place in their beloved St Ives home. Their family had to be a complete mess of emotions at the moment so was it surprising that Sir Hugo had displayed out of character kindness and courtesy towards his wife? No, probably it wasn't, in which case was Keith right, she was letting her imagination run away with her.

Of course, it was preposterous to suggest that Lady Irving would not be aware that the man who had come back from the dead was not her husband, unless they were in it together, whatever 'it' was. Maybe Bob had killed Sir Hugo in order to take his place. Certainly Sir Hugo's lifestyle was enviable. Having worked hard all his life, he was now close to retirement with a huge fortune amassed; what sane person wouldn't like the idea of living his life? She shook her head in the dark as she wove her way through the lanes to her cottage trying to clear her thoughts. She knew now she was starting to think in riddles, making no sense at all, it was best to forget it all and think again in the morning.

As it happened she had no difficultly at all in dismissing Sir Hugo and his family from her mind. As soon as she turned the key in the lock and opened the front door of Jericho Cottage, she knew something was wrong. The atmosphere was different. She couldn't put her finger on it but her heart began beating a little faster and she hurriedly climbed the stairs to the kitchen, not knowing why, but searching for … and there he was. He was stretched out in front of the Aga, apparently asleep, but for some reason she knew immediately he was dead. Orlando, her companion of eighteen years was gone. She let out a cry and knelt beside him, his body was cold but rigor mortis had not yet set in. Looking wildly around her she spied his basket. She pulled the rug free from it. It was clean and pristine for he despised his basket and never used it. Carefully she laid the blanket on the floor and lifted Orlando's body into it, wrapping him as you would wrap a baby. She rose stiffly, like an old woman, holding the body of her cat close to her and sat down on the chair, his chair, holding him close.

Nothing happened for a moment and then the tears began and once they started, she could hear herself howling with grief as she clutched the body to her. It wasn't just for the cat of course; she had loved him dearly, but it was for what he represented. The children had been small when Charlie had brought him home as a kitten. They had adored him, played with him hour after hour and Charlie had loved him too. Charlie would disappear off to his study with Orlando tucked comfortably under one arm to do 'man stuff', which meant settling down together in Charlie's big old arm chair with a whisky in front of the rugby where they fell fast asleep. She cried for Charlie, for their life in Oxford, lost; for her children grown and independent now and for Orlando dying alone without his family around him – had it hurt, had he been frightened? She cried until her head ached, her eyes stung and she was utterly exhausted. Finally, it was nearly midnight by the time, she stumbled downstairs and found a box in the cupboard under the stairs. She took it up to the kitchen table and carefully laid Orlando, blanket and all, inside it. She took one long last look at him and sealed the box, tears still running down her cheeks. Then too exhausted to do anything else, she collapsed into bed.

15

The journey to Oxford the next day seemed like it would never end. She had left home just after five in the morning and it had been torture. The weather was ludicrous for August – heavy rain, cross winds and a sullen sky that had made it necessary for headlights as far as Exeter; a journey that should have taken her five hours at the very most saw her arriving in Oxford at midday. The combination of her endless crying the previous night and such an early start meant that by the time Felicity turned in to the Banbury Road, she could barely keep her eyes open.

Gilla, her best friend from school days, lived a few streets north of where Felicity and Charlie had lived for over twenty years. Most of the houses in North Oxford were huge Victorian rambling piles but Gilla's was one of the few exceptions – a little doll's house, clearly built at the turn of the century in the garden of the huge house next door, possibly as a granny annexe or more likely as a servants' quarters.

On leaving the motorway Felicity had rung Gilla and told her she was making an unscheduled trip.

Gilla had sounded slightly flustered but had said it would be possible for her to take most of the day off work and that she would be waiting for her. Gilla owned and ran a small shop in Woodstock selling what she described as "upmarket tat" to American tourists. Despite the disparaging description of her merchandise and a rather low opinion of her customers, she was actually very clever at marketing and made a good living.

Gilla opened the door immediately as Felicity drove up her driveway. She looked wonderful, in total contrast as to how Felicity sensed she herself must appear. Gilla's riot of red curls seemed undimmed by the years; her face was unlined, her green eyes catlike and wicked as ever. Vitality sung from every pore and yet she was nearly a year older than Felicity.

'Fizzy!' she screamed, and running down the steps threw herself into Felicity's arms, hugging her tight. 'You must be exhausted,' she held her at arms length, 'you are exhausted, my poor darling you look all in. What's happened, what's up?'

'Can I come inside and have a cup of coffee before I fall over?' Felicity asked.

'Of course you can, come on.' Gilla led the way into her cosy little kitchen, put on the kettle and settled Felicity at the kitchen table. Then she sat down beside her and studied her friend in silence for a moment. 'You look ghastly,' she said.

Felicity smiled, ruefully, 'Thanks Gilla, by contrast you look absolutely wonderful.' For a moment something close to embarrassment crossed Gilla's face and her eyes slid away from Felicity. Then she looked down at her hands with a ridiculously theatrical prim expression. 'Ah,' said Felicity, knowingly, 'there's a reason for you looking so marvellous, isn't there?'

'We're not talking about me,' said Gilla, 'we're talking about you.'

'Actually,' said Felicity, 'it would be nice to have some light relief. What's going on?'

'Well,' said Gilla, immediately, obviously eager to talk, 'you remember Simon?'

'Of course I remember Simon,' said Felicity, 'he's your husband, the father of your child, my goddaughter.'

'You know he went to Hong Kong after, after …' Gilla groped for words.

'After he found you in bed with some random man young enough to be your son.'

'Thanks, Fizzy,' Gilla said, 'I was trying to find the right words to explain the unfortunate episode but you have done a brilliant job for me. A couple of years ago he was transferred back to London. I knew he was back in the country because he writes to Ellie once a year on her birthday.'

'I hadn't realised that,' said Felicity, 'I knew he sent you maintenance cheques but I didn't know he actually communicated.'

'He didn't for some years,' Gilla said, 'but once Ellie started asking about him, I wrote to him and said it would be helpful if he could be some sort of presence in her life and that's when the letters started.'

'That was nice of him.'

'Not really,' said Gilla, 'it's his duty, he is after all her father.'

'So what's changed?' Felicity asked.

Again Gilla looked embarrassed in a rather smug way. 'Well, a couple of weeks ago he asked if he could come and see us. I explained that Ellie was travelling on her gap year – she's in New Zealand at the moment working as a nanny.'

'I know,' said Felicity, 'I had a postcard from her just the other day, she sounds happy.'

'She is,' said Gilla, 'anyway I explained to Simon that she wasn't here and he asked if he could come and see me anyway.'

'I knew it,' said Felicity, 'I've always known it, so you're back together again.'

Gilla bit her lip. 'Well not exactly, actually yes, sort of.' She had the grace to blush.

'Good Lord,' said Felicity, 'you've fallen for him again haven't you?'

'I suppose I have, kind of,' Gilly admitted, 'most men are such shits, aren't they, and Simon, he's one of the good guys.'

'He certainly is,' Felicity agreed, 'you should never have let him go.'

'So you've told me periodically over the years and maybe I've listened at last. Actually, he's staying here at the moment, at any rate tonight and tomorrow night.'

'Oh my goodness, is he here now, am I interrupting?'

'No, no, when you rang, he went out. He's gone to meet a friend for lunch.'

'I'm so sorry,' said Felicity, 'I didn't know I was barging in on a love nest.'

'Hardly a love nest, darling,' said Gilla. 'I'm fifty-one and he's sixty.'

'Nonetheless,' Felicity found herself smiling properly for the first time since Orlando's death, 'I'm so happy for you, Gilla, that's great, hold on to him this time.'

'We'll see what happens, it's early days, and I don't know how Ellie is going to feel about it when she comes home.'

'I'd have thought she'd be over the moon,' Felicity said.

Gilla shrugged. 'She can't actually remember her father living with us. I know she and I have rather a strange relationship because we are very different, but we do get on rather well on a whole. She knows the odd boyfriend I've had over the years means nothing, I don't know how the dynamics would change if there were three of us permanently, not just the two of us.'

'I'd agree with you,' said Felicity, 'if the man in question wasn't Simon, but you do realise, don't you, that while you and Ellie are very different, Ellie and Simon are very alike.'

'So are you saying it might be me who feels the odd one out?' said Gilla.

Felicity laughed, 'Gilla, you'd never be the odd one out in any circumstances. No, I just mean it might be really lovely for Ellie to have someone around of like mind.'

'Instead of her stupid, scatty old mum,' Gilla said.

'No,' Felicity chose her words carefully, 'but she is very academic and very serious-minded, and so is Simon – that could be really nice for both of them.'

'If Simon and I work out that is – we'll see.'

Felicity smiled at her, fondly. 'Well, from the look of you, whatever is going on, it suits you.'

The kettle boiled and Gilla busied herself making coffee. 'So, why are you here,' she asked, 'it's lovely to see you, but it's obvious something's wrong?'

'Orlando died,' Felicity said.

'Oh Fizzy, I'm so sorry. I know how fond you were of him.'

'I was,' said Felicity, 'but it was odd, like his death triggered so much pent-up emotion. I just couldn't stop crying and I couldn't stop thinking about Charlie and our life together here.'

Gilla put out her hand and took Felicity's. 'You poor old thing, Fizzy, when did all this happen?'

'Only last night.'

'Last night, good heavens.'

'I've got Orlando in the back of the car in a cardboard box. I wondered if I could bury him in your

191

garden?'

'Of course,' said Gilla, 'but why?'

'I just needed to bring him back to Oxford, it was where he was born and spent most of his life. I obviously can't expect the new owners of our old house to put up with me digging a hole in their garden for my dead cat but I thought perhaps you would understand.'

'I do sort of,' said Gilla, who was not a natural animal lover, 'and of course we'll bury Orlando here if that's what you want, but you do worry me – Orlando was a dear but he was just a cat.'

'As I'm trying to explain he was the link,' said Felicity after a moment, 'he was the link between my life now and my life then. My Oxford cat who Charlie adored and the children played with when they were small, who sat on my lap that whole awful night when Charlie died, yet happily shared my new life in St Ives. He was a constant.'

Gilla nodded. 'I see,' she said, but Felicity sensed that she didn't.

They drank their coffee in silence for a moment. Felicity searched for a change of subject. She didn't want to talk about Orlando any more with someone who didn't really understand. 'Mel's engaged,' she said with sudden inspiration.

'Really, that's wonderful,' said Gilla, 'to that market gardener, or whatever he is?'

'Yes, Martin.'

'He's quite a lot older than her, isn't he?'

'Yes, but they are ideally suited, I'm really happy about it and even better, Mel is pregnant.'

'That's wonderful, Fizzy, I must write to her.'

'It is wonderful,' said Felicity, 'but it kind of compounds the problem.'

'And the problem is?' Gilla asked.

Felicity shrugged her shoulders. 'I'm sort of spare. James is happily married and Mel is happily engaged, I'm so pleased for both of them but they don't need me anymore. By contrast, a geriatric cat with an eating disorder and a filthy temper did need me – but not any more.' Quietly, Felicity began to cry again, she couldn't believe there were any tears left. 'I'm sorry,' she said weakly.

'Fizzy, if you can't cry with me who can you cry with? Come on, this has got to stop. What we're going to do is dig a hole for Orlando right now and then we're going to open a bottle of champagne and drink his health – action is what is needed.'

Of course Gilla was right. Half an hour later, they had dug a generous hole under the apple tree in the back of Gilla's garden. Fizzy gently placed the box in it.

'Do you want to say anything?' Gilla asked. Felicity shook her head and began filling in the hole. 'Do you remember when your hamster died?' Gilla asked. Their eyes met and they both burst into laughter. The relief was enormous, the tension eased.

'We dug up Dad's asparagus bed by mistake,' Felicity said, 'gosh, were we in trouble.'

The task finished, the two women stood back and studied the grave.

'I'll get a headstone,' said Gilla.

'You don't need to.'

'But I will. When was he born?'

'1987,' said Felicity.

'OK, so do you want it to say anything other than Orlando and his dates?' Felicity shook her head in silence, tears flooded back again. 'Come on, old girl, champagne calls.'

They went inside and washed the mud of their hands, then Gilla opened a bottle and they toasted Orlando.

'So what happens next?' Gilla asked.

'Back to Cornwall,' said Felicity.

'Not now, not today?'

'No, I thought I'd better stay overnight, I'm so exhausted.'

'You can stay in Ellie's room,' Gilla began.

'There is absolutely no way I am doing that,' said Felicity firmly, 'not with Simon here. I'll book myself into the Old Parsonage if they have a room free.'

'You can't stay in a hotel, I'd feel awful.'

'Gilla,' said Felicity. 'I'm not staying here, alright! Let's have lunch together and then I'll be on my way. I'll quite enjoy a little hotel luxury.'

'Are you sure you should be going back to Cornwall at all?'

'We're not starting that again are we?' Felicity asked.

'It's just that whenever disaster strikes, you always come back here, which is lovely, but it makes me wonder whether St Ives really is home?'

'St Ives really is home,' said Felicity, 'but there is no friend like an old friend. It was an instinctive thing this morning, getting in the car and driving here, it was barely a conscious thought, it was just something that had to be done – bringing Orlando back to Oxford.'

'You're nowhere near getting over Charlie, are you?' Gilla said, suddenly.

Tears welled into Felicity's eyes immediately. 'No,' she said, 'I think it's because I've spent most of the last three years in denial. Because he lied about his past I have been telling myself that grieving for him wasn't appropriate in view of the fact he wasn't the man I thought he was – but, Gilla, he was a lovely person, a good father, a good husband, he was so funny, so lovable ...'

'He'd certainly be a tough act to follow, old Charlie,' Gilla conceded, 'but while he will always be a precious part of your life, the main part of your life, you are going to have to move forward now. You can't change the past, you can only change the future and you deserve a happy future, Fizzy, you really do. It's time to move on.'

The Old Parsonage Hotel offered just the sort of comfort Felicity needed – pampering without fuss.

After a scalding hot shower, she sank into a deliciously soft bed and slept the afternoon away. She woke to a familiar sound, so familiar that for a moment she was completely disorientated. It was Thursday evening – bell-ringing practice in St Giles Church. The sound of the bells had been a constant part of the fabric of her married life, yet lying in the cosy bed, the sound brought only comfort, not sorrow and made her smile – it was quite a contrast to the sound of seagulls. The temptation to stay tucked up was overwhelming, but through the curtains she could see it was a beautiful evening and galvanising herself into action, she got up and dressed in jeans and a T-shirt. It was six o'clock, time for a walk before dinner and there was no question as to where would be her destination. She slipped out of the front door of the Old Parsonage and cut through the churchyard of St Giles Church, the bells ringing in her ears, moments later she stood on the kerb of the Woodstock Road. On the opposite side of the road was the little newsagents, a little further up the Radcliffe Infirmary. She looked at the lamppost to the left of her and moved a few feet nearer to it. This was the exact spot where Charlie had died. Twice before, standing here, she had seen a vision of his death but she knew today that would not be the case, that was over, she was simply here to pay her respects.

Strangely, the place now seemed to hold no special significance for her and having stood uncertainly for a moment or two, she walked back through the churchyard, across the Banbury Road and into the Parks. The Parks were where she and Charlie had learnt to love one another, talking endlessly on the benches, sitting on the grass with a picnic watching cricket matches on a Sunday afternoon, drifting down the Cherwell in a punt. This is where she could remember him best, his blonde hair flopping in his eyes, just like his grandson; witty clever talk masking a vulnerability she had found irresistible. During August there were no students around just a few tourists, and one or two families picnicking with small children, now packing up ready for bathtime and bedtime. She walked and remembered and was soothed by it. She walked for over an hour and by the time she was back at the bar of the Old Parsonage, while she felt no happier, she felt a great deal calmer and more at ease with herself.

The following couple of weeks were hectic ones for Felicity. She finished her paintings and sent them off to the publisher and then there were one or two amendments to make. Jamie and family had arrived and the house was in turmoil with endless meals to cook, but it was wonderful to have them there and to see the boys. The weather held and they swam and played on the beach every day. By the time they left, it was the end of the first week of September, the holidaymakers had all gone now, buckets and spades packed away, shrimping nets too and they had been replaced by older visitors who were no longer subject to the tyranny of the school term. The St Ives September Festival was well under way with art exhibitions, concerts in the church and all manner of activities around the town. It was a stimulating creative period and anxious to keep her melancholy thoughts at bay, Felicity made sure she was fully occupied. One evening she went to an art exhibition on the Wharf. The art was not to her taste, aggressive, street art, full of anger and resentment; she didn't like it at all but part of the proceeds were being donated to the Children's Hospice so she thought she should attend. She had just collected an extremely revolting glass of red wine when across the room she spotted Keith Penrose. He saw her at the same moment waved his hand in welcome and she threaded her way through the crowd towards him.

He smiled warmly at her and nodded at the art. 'This it truly terrible, isn't it?'

'I'm afraid I have to agree with you,' she said, smiling too. 'How are you?'

'Pretty good, and you too, I hope. You've been very quiet. I was expecting to be plagued with your theories about the Irvings morning, noon and night until I did something about them.'

'I've had one or two other things on my mind,' said Felicity.

'Oh, what's up, nothing wrong?'

Felicity hesitated, feeling a little foolish. 'Well, you'll think I'm stupid,' she said, 'but I lost my cat recently. Actually it was the night I rang you from the Mount. I got back here to find he had died.'

'The monster marmalade cat?' Keith asked. Felicity nodded, pleased that he had remembered Orlando. 'I'm sorry,' he said, 'it's always hard to lose an animal, I hate it.'

'It's just that this one was special,' she said, 'he had been with me for so long.'

'While the children were young and your husband was still alive,' Keith finished for her.

'Exactly,' she said, grateful for his understanding. 'It sort of bought it all back. I went up to Oxford to bury him and I found that hard too, though I'm glad to be back. Then my son and his family came to stay, and well, here we are. Oh, and I forget to mention,' she said, 'my daughter, Mel, is engaged.'

'Congratulations,' said Keith, 'who is the lucky chap?'

'Martin Tregonning, you remember him?'

Keith frowned for a moment. 'That was your fellow conspirator, the one who kept unlawfully breaking into houses with you.'

'Don't exaggerate, it was only the once, into Boswithey and we were entirely justified.'

'He's a nice chap as I remember, quite a bit older than her though, I would have thought.'

'She needs a steady hand, she is a very strong character.'

'She doesn't take after her mother then,' said Keith, grinning.

'Now, now, Chief Inspector, I've been no trouble at all of late as you've just pointed out ...' she hesitated, always finding the contrast between her daughter and his very difficult to handle. 'How's Carly?' she asked.

'Good,' said Keith, 'she's just had another check up and they don't want to see her again for three months this time.'

'That's marvellous,' said Felicity, 'you must be so relieved.'

'We are,' said Keith. 'We've agreed, all three of us, to make a real effort to put this thing behind us for the next three months and just concentrate on the present.'

'That's what I need to do,' said Felicity, 'the "what-ifs" get you nowhere, do they?'

Keith nodded his head in agreement. 'It's getting awfully crowded; do you fancy a quick glass of wine at the Sloop? I've got to get home, I mustn't be too long, but I wanted to just talk to you about the Irvings.'

'Don't tell me you've come around to my way of thinking?' said Felicity.

'I'll tell you all about it in a minute. Come on, let's get out of here, don't drink that wine it's terrible.'

There was a log fire in the public bar, Keith fetched glasses of wine and they sat down in the corner, by the fire, there was no one else about.

'Thanks,' said Felicity.

'Well,' said Keith, raising his glass, 'here's to a loyal friend, to Orlando.'

'Thank you,' said Felicity, genuinely touched, 'to Orlando.'

They put down their glasses and regarded one another in silence for a moment.

'It will get better, I promise,' Keith said gently.

'What?' Felicity asked.

He shrugged his shoulders, 'Life – you've had the most huge adjustments to make over the last few years, but one of these days you'll wake up and feel really positive about your future and soon after that you will learn to be happy again.'

'You know,' said Felicity, 'for a policeman you're really rather a nice man.'

'I'll take that as a compliment,' said Keith. 'Now, about the Irvings, well not so much about the Irvings more about Bob Barnes. Tresco Estate has reported him as a missing person.'

'Heavens, when did that happen?'

'Earlier this week,' said Keith, 'apparently he has done a bunk before, they are quite used to his odd ways and initially thought nothing of it. This time he's gone away in August, which is unusual in itself and he just hasn't come back. The most he's ever been away before is for a week or two so now they're worried,' Keith confirmed, 'and so am I.'

'And do you think there's a link to the Irvings?'

'I didn't,' said Keith, 'I thought you were

exaggerating but Tresco e-mailed me a photograph of Bob unloading plants on the quay. It was an atmospheric shot, probably taken for a newspaper, I imagine, and not very distinct. However I had it enlarged and I do see what you mean, he is absolutely a dead ringer for Sir Hugo – no, he is Sir Hugo, except for the ponytail and the rather outlandish clothes.'

'I told you,' said Felicity.

'And I'm acknowledging you're right, Mrs Paradise.'

'So what are you going to do about it?' Felicity asked.

'I'm going up to London tomorrow to see the Irvings. I've checked the dates and you were right, Bob disappeared five days before Hugo reappeared and that is fairly odd on two counts – firstly that Bob seems to have disappeared off the face of the earth and secondly that Sir Hugo's reappearance story is a bit weak, to put it mildly.'

'This really is a missing person's saga, isn't it,' said Felicity. 'People keep disappearing at the drop of a hat and then reappearing without any help from any of us.'

'You're right, I do feel extremely ineffectual. I know we found Marianna's killer and that was very important, but like everything else that's happened in this case I had no influence at all – it's very bad for the ego.'

'So,' said Felicity, smiling wickedly, 'now is your chance to make a difference, now is your chance to take notice of my idea and check out Sir Hugo.'

'That's what I'm going to do, though where it will get me heaven only knows.'

'It wasn't the closeness of the dates, it wasn't even that Sir Hugo's story is a bit thin because I didn't know that – it was the kindness of his gesture when Lady Irving stumbled, it just wasn't something that Sir Hugo would have done.'

'But was it something that Bob Barnes would have done?' Keith asked.

'Well you know more about him that I do, I expect,' said Felicity, 'I've only had some very sketchy secondhand information from Sarah.'

'I think he probably is a fairly gentle fellow, certainly despite his reclusive nature he doesn't have any bad habits, he's not a heavy drinker, he's never aggressive, never upsets anyone, either fellow workers or the public. They reckon at the Estate Office he had a pretty miserable childhood. He was in a children's home for most of it, and that as a result has never found it easy to mix socially with people in the normal way. He loves plants and animals more than people.'

'No doubt you'll have the case all wrapped up by this time tomorrow, Chief Inspector,' Felicity said, smiling.

'Well, let's hope so otherwise poor old Bob Barnes is going to join the thick file of missing persons who, despite our best efforts, we never find.'

'Are there a lot?' Felicity asked, curiously.

'Yes, and the number is increasing – teenage runaways of course, but also apparently stable people; older people with families, husbands and wives, they disappear too. There is usually a cause – money, a collapsed relationship – but not always. The pressure of life I think is probably the main culprit.'

'Well as you say,' said Felicity, 'let's hope Bob Barnes isn't going to join the rest of them.'

16

Keith Penrose found he was surprisingly nervous as he sat in the back of the taxicab on the way from Paddington Station to Notting Hill. It was just after ten o'clock; he had caught the early train, but had not telephoned ahead. He had told no one except Felicity of his intended interview, not his super, not the Met and least of all, the Irvings. Surprise was his only weapon, that and Miles – he had a feeling the boy would find it difficult to lie to him. They had got on well in Romania, shared something important. If there was something going on in the Irving house, Keith had a feeling that Miles would find it hard to keep it from him. Keith was also aware that he was running a considerable risk personally. Sir Hugo Irving was a formidable man with huge influence. If Keith got this wrong, if the man living with Lady Irving really was her husband, then the repercussions of accusing him of being otherwise could be huge. Keith could imagine a very unpleasant scene unfolding with his superior officers being left unamused, but his instincts told him that he was on the right track and equally Felicity Paradise thought he was too and that counted for something. Despite her wilder moments and flights of fancy, she had an unerring way of judging accurately a situation and people's reaction to it. She didn't believe that Sir Hugo had come back from the dead and that was good enough for him, he just had to hope that this time she had not got it wrong.

Thirty minutes later in another taxi heading back to Paddington, he was sure that she was right, something wasn't right, but how to prove it.

The door had been opened by the Irvings' jolly housekeeper, who was not so jolly today. 'I know you,' she said accusingly, 'you're that policeman. What do you want?'

'Are they in?' He had asked.

'Who?'

Nerves had worn his patience paper thin. 'The Irvings, the people you work for, the owners of this house, you remember them?'

'There's no need to get lippy with me, boy,' she said. 'They're not here.'

'Not even Miles?'

'Not even Master Miles.'

'Where are they?' Keith had asked.

'I have no idea.'

'But you must have, you're the housekeeper. They wouldn't go off without telling you where they had gone.'

'I look after this house and the family when they are here. When they are not here, it is none of my business where they go … or yours,' she added, hands on hips now.

'When did they go?' Keith asked.

'Last week sometime, Tuesday or Wednesday as I recall.'

'Have they gone to their holiday home in Crete?'

'I don't know,' she replied, 'I've told you that.'

'And when are you expecting them back?'

'I don't know that either. They'll be back here when they're good and ready.'

'Is there anything else you can tell me?'

'Nope.'

'Well,' said Keith, sarcastically, 'thank you very much indeed for your co-operation.'

'That's a pleasure, boy,' she said but it was impossible to tell from her expression whether her words were as ironic as they sounded.

Defeated, Keith started to leave and then on impulse turned back. 'Sir Hugo,' he said, 'do you find him greatly changed since his disappearance?'

Immediately Keith sensed a wariness. 'What do you mean by that?' she demanded.

'He went through a considerable ordeal; it must be very frightening to lose a part of your life like that. I just wondered how it has affected him and how he is behaving now he's back with the family.'

'Same as always.'

'Are you sure?' Keith asked.

'Absolutely.'

'And have you ever heard of a man called Bob Barnes?'

Again the wariness. 'I've never heard of him,' she said.

'What is your name?' Keith asked.

'Mary Peters,' was the reply.

'Well, Mary Peters,' said Keith, 'I don't think you're being entirely honest with me.' She looked unabashed. 'You're not planning on going anywhere, are you, or disappearing on me, too?'

'No boy, I'm here until the family get back.'

'Well, just make sure that you are, because I'll be along to see you again I don't doubt.'

She knew something, Keith was sure of that as he leaned back in the taxi. It was all so frustrating. He dialled Jack Curnow's number and explained the position.

'What now then, boss?' Jack asked.

'Do some digging, talk to the Met, they interviewed the accountant and Sir Hugo's personal assistant in charge of his business affairs, I'd like to speak to one of them.'

'Are you staying in London then?'

'No, no, just on the phone, I'm on my way back to Cornwall now. Also, do some digging into Sir Hugo's past again. I know the Met covered the ground, but for those two men to look so alike there has to be a family link. Dig and keep digging, Jack, oh and incidentally, can you do some airport checking and see if the Irvings have flown anywhere in the last week?'

'Anything else?' Jack asked, dryly.

'That'll do for now – see what you can put together by the time I get back to Truro.'

By the time Keith boarded his train, Jack had furnished him with the name and telephone number of Sir Hugo's accountant and chief executive – a man by the name of David Blackman. From experience, Keith knew that the network coverage on his mobile worked as far as Newbury but further west was decidedly patchy for the rest of the journey. He might as well strike while he could, so he telephoned the number straight away, as the train pulled out of Paddington Station. Anxious not to be overheard, he stood between two carriages, swaying uncomfortably and having to shout to make himself understood. It was not an ideal way to conduct an interview.

David Blackman sounded a pleasant enough man and was very helpful, too, although he too had no idea where the Irvings were, other than that they were on holiday.

'But surely,' said Keith, 'Sir Hugo would have left a contact number for you of all people?'

'As a matter of fact, he didn't. He has never liked mobile phones and considers them a sloppy way in which to do business. He likes his business to run like a well-oiled machine – his words – and considers that he should be dispensable, particularly on holiday.'

'Has he taken up the reins of the business again now he is back?' Keith asked.

'Not really,' said David Blackman, 'nor is he intending to do so. When he disappeared the plans we had set in place to run the group should anything happen to him worked seamlessly. If you noticed, Chief Inspector,' the man spoke with considerable pride, 'on Sir Hugo's disappearance there was only a very temporary blip in the shares of Irving Holdings and within a couple of weeks they were slightly up on where they had been before his disappearance. Plans were already being drawn up for the shareholding to be passed to Lady Irving and their son when Sir Hugo reappeared and since he has returned, he has continued to leave the running of the Group to us. As he said, we appear to be doing such an excellent job why disturb things?'

'That doesn't sound very like him,' said Keith, 'are you saying he's retired?'

'I think his ordeal has taken its toll,' David replied, diplomatically. 'And then there was the terrible business of the dead girl in the family's home at St Ives. I don't think he has decided about his future yet, but ...' the man hesitated.

'But what?' Keith asked.

'Well, it's a private matter really, not one to discuss with anyone.'

'I'm struggling here, Mr Blackman, if you have

anything to tell me you'd better do it now, because I am losing patience with this family.'

'He's asked us to continue with the transfer of his shareholding to his wife and son. I think having faced his own immortality it made him feel that it was time to take a back seat – again, those were his words .'

'And have you seen much of him since he came back?'

'Hardly at all,' David Blackman said. 'He came into the office to sign some papers with Lady Irving, but mostly we've dealt with her. As she explained, he is very tired at the moment, head injuries make you tired apparently.'

'And have you noticed anything odd about him?'

There was a pause. 'Not really Chief Inspector, not considering what he's been through.'

'You are sure that the man who came in to sign papers with his wife was Sir Hugo?'

'What are you implying?' said David Blackman, sounding genuinely shocked. 'Of course it was Sir Hugo.'

'So you have no reason to suppose it was an impostor, someone pretending to be Sir Hugo?'

'Of course not.'

'And why was that?'

'Because he looked like Sir Hugo, talked like Sir Hugo and was with Lady Irving. Why would I possibly imagine him to be an impostor? I don't understand what you're saying, Chief Inspector.'

'Neither do I,' Keith replied, 'and that's the

trouble.'

Maggie Curnow was trying very hard, very hard indeed, but all her good resolutions were flying out of the window. It was their third wedding anniversary and rather than go out this year, she and Jack had decided to celebrate quietly at home. Maggie had cooked roast chicken, Jack's favourite, followed even more indulgently by sticky toffee pudding. She had bought champagne, though she herself, would only have a sip of course. She had put fresh flowers on the table and laid it carefully – it looked lovely. It was now nearly nine o'clock, the chicken had dried out and Jack was still at the station. It had been half past seven when she had telephoned him and he said he would be home directly – she was not going to call again. It was all very well for Chief Inspector bloody Penrose to say she should make a life for herself but who was she expected to celebrate her wedding anniversary with other than her husband? How many more wedding anniversaries would she be spending alone? She was depressed rather than angry. All that food spoiled, all those loving preparations for nothing. She turned off the lights in the dining room, the oven in the kitchen and wearily climbed the stairs to bed.

It was nearly half past nine by the time Jack Curnow burst into Keith's office. 'I've got it!' he said, triumphantly.

Keith had been sitting blurry-eyed behind his desk being extremely ineffectual. He was dead tired and his brain seemed to have completely given out, but as Jack came through the door he was suddenly alert.

'What have you got for me then, Jack?' Jack had an expression of triumph on his face.

'You're going to like this, boss,' he said.

'Go on then, confound me,' said Keith.

'In 1946 in Bradford identical twin boys were born to a seventeen year old single woman by the name of Betty Abercrombie. The boys were named Robert and William and placed in the care of the local authority by the girl, who either didn't want them or couldn't care for them. When the boys were only a few days old.' Jack paused, dramatically, 'One of them was taken for adoption by a Mr and Mrs John Irving of Bingley, West Yorkshire.' Keith whistled through his teeth.

'And I assume the boy they took was William.'

'That's right,' said Jack, 'they took William home and renamed him Hugh after John's father, I imagine, who was certainly of the same name. Robert was never adopted. Those were the days when if you started out life in a children's home and were not adopted, that's where you stayed.'

Keith leaned forward in his chair, frowning. 'But how come he's not Robert Abercrombie?'

'I've no idea,' said Jack, 'but it's what has made

my life particularly difficult. Clearly at some time Bob changed his name. I imagine that he must have been fairly bitter – first because his mother rejected him at birth and then because the Irvings chose his brother and not him.'

'Assuming of course that he knew all that,' Keith interrupted, 'we don't know for certain that either boy was aware he had a brother, do we?'

'Any member of staff who was at the children's home, which incidentally closed down about twenty years ago, at the time of the Abercrombie boys' birth will be long dead I imagine, so I have no one to speak to with any first-hand knowledge, but the records are all there, so it is not unreasonable to assume that both boys were aware of their origins. Sir Hugo was presumably told by his parents and for Bob, living on at the children's home, it was probably common knowledge.'

'You're not necessarily right about Hugo,' Keith said, 'after all, years later he took it upon himself not to divulge to his own adopted son the boy's true origins.'

'I wonder why that was?' Jack said. 'You would have thought, bearing in mind his own family history, he would have been particularly anxious to do the right thing by Miles. Maybe he had a bad experience being told of his own adoption.'

'It could be,' said Keith, slowly, 'or alternatively, knowing he had a brother and not being able to live with him could have made him feel that it would have been better not to have known any details of his adoption.'

'Possibly,' Jack agreed.

'I assume we have no idea whether the brothers have ever met?'

'We have no idea; there is no evidence of any contact between them apart from being born and spending a few weeks of their life together.'

'How very sad,' said Keith, 'I suppose the Irvings could only afford one child. The father was a miner, I believe?'

Jack nodded. 'Those were the days when no one thought twice about splitting up siblings, even, dear God, identical twins. Strange how life repeats itself, it's like Miles and his sister all over again,' said Jack.

The two men were silent for a moment, both lost in thought. 'So where do you think that leaves us?' Jack asked, at last.

'Bob Barnes is clearly Robert Abercrombie and Hugo Irving is clearly William Abercrombie but which one of them is squiring around Lady Irving at this moment, God only knows and where they are – God only knows that too. I think we need to look at this with a clear mind in the morning.'

'I would be grateful, sir,' said Jack, 'I'm afraid I've probably just undone all the good you did the other day when you spoke to Maggie.'

'Why's that?' Keith asked.

'It's our wedding anniversary today.'

'You should have said.' Keith looked appalled.

'You shouldn't have spent the evening here on your wedding anniversary.'

'I just had to get to the bottom of it, boss. Once I discovered that the Irvings had adopted their son, I had to find out who he was and when I discovered he was one of twins, well …'

'The thrill of the chase,' Keith said smiling at him.

'That's it, sir, exactly, I couldn't let it rest could I, not until I'd got it straight in my mind.'

'You're a very good policeman, Jack,' Keith said.

'But not a very good husband.'

'I'm afraid the two often don't go together. Don't worry, she'll come round. Tell her you've cracked the case again. It's true, God knows, you've been a damn sight more useful on this one than I've been. I'm losing my touch I think.'

'Not true, boss, but I think we're getting somewhere at last.'

'I hope you're right Jack, I do hope you are.'

17

Superintendent George Staple was a straightforward, honest, reliable man. His meteoric rise through the police force had been achieved by fair means not foul. There were no skeletons in his cupboard; honesty was his trademark, truth, his religion. He would defend to the hilt the misdemeanours and mistakes of his officers if they were straight with him. If they lied or were even economical with the truth, they were out, sidelined before they hardly knew what had happened to them – all of which was making this morning's meeting with Keith Penrose particularly uncomfortable. George liked Keith. He was an old-fashioned copper, a decent man with more compassion and tolerance of human frailty than George himself possessed, which was probably why he was sitting in the superintendent's chair and Keith Penrose had only just made it up to Chief Inspector a few years before retirement. It was amazing that all his years in the force had not blunted the basic kindness in Keith's nature, which in today's more brutal world, many mistook for weakness.

Keith had brought him the breakthrough George knew was inevitable. There was something of the terrier about Keith Penrose, he worried a problem until he solved it, he never gave up. It was the solution to the problem that George hoped he would never find, but in his heart he knew he would. As always Keith was completely frank – he reckoned he had got somewhere at last with the Irving case but it was no thanks to him but to his Sergeant Jack Curnow. George listened with mounting apprehension while Keith described the story of the twins.

'So sir,' Keith said, 'once I've found him again I'd like to call in Sir Hugo for questioning in the belief that what we'll uncover is the fact that he's really Bob Barnes.'

George took a deep breath. 'I'd like you to drop it, Keith.'

'What?' Keith stared at his boss in disbelief.

'I said, I'd like you to drop it,' George repeated, 'and that's an end to it, Keith. I don't want to explain to you why, I just want you to accept what I'm saying as an instruction – drop it, forget it, move on.'

'I can't do that, sir,' Keith said.

'You can if you want to keep your job.'

'But why?' Keith asked, he had stood up now and was pacing the room. George could feel the frustration dripping off him, and was full of sympathy but he certainly couldn't afford to show it. 'It's my belief sir, that there may well be another murder involved with this Irving case. If Bob Barnes is impersonating his brother, there is a distinct possibility that he may have killed him. Living the life of Sir Hugo Irving has to be preferable to being a handyman on Tresco. If he is an impostor then Lady Irving is certainly involved and maybe even the son, Miles. There is certainly a conspiracy to defraud, at the very least, but my instincts tell me that if the man sharing Lady Irving's bed is Bob Barnes, then between them they murdered Hugo Irving.'

'Sit down, Keith,' George said wearily. Keith did as he was told. He had great respect for George Staple, but he didn't like the expression he saw on his boss's face – he was being less than frank and that was something Keith had never come across before in his long association with the man.

'We've worked together for many years Keith, right?' Keith nodded. 'I've tried always to be fair and straightforward, but I will not be disregarded by anyone, even you. I'm not asking you, or suggesting, I'm simply telling you to drop this. It is an instruction, I don't expect you to query it and I certainly don't expect you to disobey it. As far as I am concerned, the matter is now closed.'

'But Sir Hugo Irving is a powerful public figure – the wrong man in his job could cause untold damage to the economy, to the Stock Market, never mind making us look like a lot of bloody fools for not spotting it.'

'I don't care if Sir Hugo Irving turns out to be Father Christmas, Keith. I've asked you to drop it, the subject is now closed. Is there anything else you'd like to discuss with me?'

'Meet you in the Globe in half an hour,' Keith barked down the telephone to Jack Curnow.

'What, the Globe pub, sir?'

'Yes, of course the Globe pub,' Keith replied, tetchily.

Keith Penrose liked his wine, Jack knew he was something of a wine buff, but he never drank on duty and rarely during the day. Jack glanced at his watch – it was only just after midday. This had to be a first – what on earth had happened?

When Jack arrived at the Globe, Keith was already sitting morosely in the corner nursing a pint. Jack collected one himself and sat down opposite his boss. 'What's up, sir?' he asked.

'We've been told to drop the case,' Keith said.

'The Irving case?'

Keith nodded.

'But that's ridiculous we're just starting to get somewhere.'

'I know, I know, there's something going on though God knows what. Staple was absolutely insistent, he got quite hot under the collar, threatened me with my job if I so much as attempted to pursue our enquiries.'

'Jesus,' said Jack, 'what's that all about then, sir?'

Keith looked up at Jack for the first time. 'I just don't know, Jack, but whatever it is, it's wrong. As I said to the super, if it is Bob Barnes impersonating his brother then the chances are he killed Hugo. Effectively, by ignoring the facts you uncovered last night, we are being implicated in a possible murder.'

'You reckon Bob murdered Sir Hugo?' Jack asked.

'I don't know,' Keith answered frankly. 'I have absolutely no idea, but there is certainly a motive there.'

'But surely,' said Jack, 'if it is Bob Barnes who is impersonating Sir Hugo, Lady Irving would have come forward and told us, or Miles, or the housekeeper, or someone close to them? Bob Barnes can't have any understanding of the intricacies of Sir Hugo's business, surely – he would give himself away in seconds.'

'Exactly,' said Keith, 'that's what has made me even more anxious. When I spoke to the accountant, it appears that Sir Hugo is pulling out of his business interests using the excuse of his accident to retire. The accountant as good as admitted that most of his dealings in recent weeks have been with Lady Irving and he had only seen Sir Hugo once to sign some papers. If Lady Irving was in on the plot and Miles too, maybe even the housekeeper – she certainly wasn't very friendly towards me – they could probably fool the rest of the world by playing a low profile and keeping their heads down. Even if they officially retire

Hugo, there will be a colossal amount of money to live on. The whole thing stinks.' Keith took a long swig of his beer, replacing the glass none too gently on the table. Jack had never seen his boss like this before.

'Well whatever our views, sir, we're just going to have to go along with it, aren't we.'

'Are we?' Keith glared at him.

'Yes, boss, you know we are. Superintendent Staple has threatened you with your job, it's not worth it. Whatever his reasons, we just have to accept it and get on with the next case.'

'You sound like him,' Keith said, morosely. 'I've worked with him for years, Jack, and I've never known him like this. He is the most straightforward man you could ever wish to meet, but he wasn't being straight with me this morning and apart from anything else, I find it bloody insulting. Maybe he has good reason – though what I can't imagine – for dropping the case, but if so, the least he could do is share it with me.'

'Maybe he can't, maybe his hands are tied for some reason.'

'Oh come on, Jack, this is real life, not some bloody police drama on TV. Whatever it is he can surely share it with me.'

'I think we're going to have to move on from this one, sir,' Jack said gently.

Barbara echoed the same sentiments later that evening. Keith had left work early unable to settle to anything. He had taken Buster, his rescue greyhound, for a long walk, longer than was really comfortable for Buster's poor old arthritic joints. Barbara found him nursing a cup of tea at the kitchen table. Buster was too exhausted to even raise his head when his mistress came in.

'What have you done to that poor dog, Keith?' she asked.

Keith sighed. 'I've took him for much too long a walk, I've doubled up on his pills, fetched him a hot water bottle and he seems quite settled now. Sorry, I should have had more sense.'

'So what's up with you?'

Keith filled her in on the developments of the day.

'Well there isn't much to say is there, Keith? You're just going to have to do what the super says.'

'I can't just let it go,' Keith said, 'I really can't.'

Barbara let out an audible sigh and filled the kettle. 'How many years have you worked with George Staple?'

'Most of my working life,' Keith said, 'over thirty years anyway.'

'And do you trust him?'

'Of course.'

'And like him?'

'Yes.'

'Do you believe him to be fair and honest?'

'Normally,' Keith said.

'And is he, or is he not, your boss?'

'Where's all this leading,' Keith asked.

'To that old-fashioned word, trust,' said Barbara. 'Do you want another cup of tea?'

'Yes, please,' Keith said.

'You have to trust him, Keith. For some reason, it is not appropriate for this case to be pursued and you just have to trust the powers that be know what they're talking about.'

'It's trust that's upsetting me,' said Keith, 'if there's a reason we can't pursue the Irving case then why couldn't George trust me enough to tell me what it was?'

'Ah,' said Barbara, 'so that's what is really upsetting you.'

Keith nodded. 'Yes, I suppose you're right. I felt like a kid talking to a grown up; you know the sort of thing – "You're not to climb that apple tree again. Why not Dad?" "Because I say so".'

'Well my advice is just to forget it, Keith. Do you want a biscuit with your tea?'

It was Miles he couldn't get out of his mind. A little boy dumped into an orphanage, separated from his sister, raised in ignorance as to his background, to know his sister only for moments and then to find her dead body and now he was in the centre of another kind of mess. It was over a solitary breakfast, Barbara having left early for a planning meeting, that Keith suddenly remembered that he had Miles's mobile number; Miles had given it to him at Bucharest Airport. He toyed with what he was going to say and decided that the simplest thing was to simply ask how he was doing and see if anything emerged. The number rang and then the answerphone cut in.

'Hello, Miles. It's Keith Penrose here. I was just ringing to see how you were getting on. Give me a call if you've got a moment.' With a sigh, Keith stood up put on his jacket, slipped his phone into his pocket and headed for the back door. He was defeated. There really was, he recognised, nothing more he could do.

Henry and Ursula Sinclair were proving delightful new friends for Felicity. They had met several times during the September Festival at one concert or another. Felicity had invited them to dinner and now they were reciprocating. They were her sort of people, very reminiscent of the slightly wacky academics she and Charlie had known in North Oxford. Dinner had comprised of a big peasant stew mopped up with garlic bread and lubricated with generous quantities of red wine. There were just the three of them and Archie and their devotion to Archie was another dimension to the relationship. They completely understood her apparent inability to come to terms with Orlando's death. All sorts of people, even Annie, had suggested a replacement cat or a little dog. Only the Sinclairs seemed to recognise that this was not possible at the moment, Orlando was irreplaceable – first she had to learn to live without him before even considering sharing her life with another four-legged friend.

The Sinclairs lived in Richmond Place, a delightful row of Victorian terraced houses, with a little garden at the front which looked out over St Ives Bay. It was a balmy evening and Henry suggested that they should take their coffee and some sloe gin out onto the terrace. Felicity knew she should refuse the sloe gin but it was the first evening she had started to feel normal since Orlando's death and she couldn't see how a little too much booze could do her any harm, she only had to walk home.

'So,' said Ursula as they settled down round the table, 'the Irvings seem to be out of the news at last. I did feel sorry for them. I know they've always courted publicity in the past, but when something terrible happens you do wish the media would leave them alone.'

Felicity's tongue was loosened by alcohol. 'I think,' she said, 'that the man who has come back as Sir Hugo with amnesia is an impostor.'

'Really,' said Henry, 'do you have any inside knowledge to support this or is it just a theory?' He was smiling at her indulgently over the top of his half moon spectacles.

'Both,' said Felicity, 'I do have a friend in the police force but ...' and then she told them the whole story of Bob Barnes and his disappearance to coincide with Sir Hugo's reappearance.

'And your policeman friend wasn't interested?' Ursula said.

'Not even slightly,' Felicity said, 'he's used to my hare-brained ideas but he said this was a bridge too far.'

'I was at Cambridge with Hugo Irving,' Henry said.

'Were you,' said Felicity, 'you've never mentioned it before?'

'Well, I never knew him, at least never spoke to him, knew of him but we were reading different subjects at different colleges and I don't even think we were in the same year, but he was someone who made quite a stir even then.'

'In what way?' Felicity asked.

'Oh, he was something of a lefty in those days, always arguing the toss in one debating society or another.'

'A communist?' Felicity asked.

'Probably, certainly a far cry from someone who was to go on to be one of the West's most successful capitalists. Ironic really, but then we all have madcap ideas when we are young, don't we?'

'Was he very politically active then?'

'No, I wouldn't say very politically active, but his views were fairly extreme and he made a bit of a name for himself. He was a show off even then, though he wasn't Hugo, he was simply Hugh in those days.'

'Really?' said Felicity.

'Yes, I think that Hugo must have coincided with his change of politics. His father was a miner, you know, and Hugo doesn't exactly sound like the name of a miner's son, does it?'

'I suppose not,' said Felicity, 'odd though for such a definite person to go from one extreme to another.'

'Money corrupts,' Ursula said, 'if people have the knack of earning it,' she smiled sweetly at Henry. 'We've never been able to do it but there are people who do, Hugo being one of them. I suppose you get corrupted it by it in the end, it becomes the most important thing, at least for some people.'

'Maybe he was a spy,' said Felicity and then instantly felt foolish, the sloe gin was very strong.

Henry laughed. 'What makes you say that?'

'Well, Cambridge being the hotbed of KGB recruitment.'

'I know I'm an old codger but this was a bit after Philby and Blunt and that lot.'

'Bet the Russians were still sniffing around though,' said Felicity, 'they clearly considered that Cambridge was a very rich seam.'

'Maybe,' said Henry, 'I can't say anybody ever approached me about being a spy. I'd have quite liked all that – Martinis shaken or was it stirred?'

'Darling,' said Ursula, fondly, 'I don't think a boffin in the science lab would have been an obvious candidate for recruitment.'

Henry regarded her over his glasses. 'I'd have

thought my cover would have been excellent, no one would ever have guessed I was really a secret agent.'

'That's very true,' said Ursula dryly.

They had met quite by chance at Saturday's Farmers' Market in Truro. Keith had been sent out with a shopping list, Felicity was in town to meet Mel for lunch later.

'I've been meaning to ring you,' said Keith, apologetically. 'I felt I owed you an explanation but it's difficult … how about a coffee?'

'I'd like that,' said Felicity.

Bags stowed under the table, coffee ordered, they sat down in the open air on the Piazza.

'I love this time of year,' said Keith, 'it's a beautiful day but there's that little chill in the air. It's perfect walking weather – I love walking, but Barbara's not keen.'

'Charlie and I used to walk a lot,' Felicity said, 'the Lake District, Scotland – we did the Ridgeway once, all forty miles in one go, we were absolutely knackered by the end of it, we did Hadrian's Wall too, that was wonderful – have you done that?'

'I haven't done anything,' said Keith, 'I do bits of the Coastal path from time to time, but as I said, Barbara isn't keen and it's not much fun on your own. Anyway, I never have the time,' he hesitated. 'About the whole Irving thing – the case is closed, my super is satisfied with how things stand so therefore I am too.'

'I had dinner the other night with the Sinclairs.' Keith frowned. 'You know Henry and Ursula Sinclair who have Archie.'

'Of course, yes,' said Keith.

'We had far too much to drink and were mulling over the whole thing. As you know they feel quite involved because Archie found not only Sir Hugo's discarded beachwear, but also Anya.'

'I remember it well,' said Keith.

'Henry Sinclair was at Cambridge with Hugo, something I didn't know before. Henry said Hugo was very political and had fairly extreme left-winged principles, almost a communist, I think. By the end of the evening, given that we had drunk quite a lot of sloe gin, I decided that Sir Hugo was a spy.'

'Well it would fit in with his untimely disappearance,' said Keith, 'but not with his reappearance.'

'Ah,' said Felicity, 'but there, of course, we come full circle because I don't think Sir Hugo has reappeared. I think the man on Lady Irving's arm is Bob. So maybe Sir Hugo was bumped off by the KGB and Bob has taken his place.'

'There you go again!' said Keith, smiling.

Felicity laid a hand on his arm. 'I am only joking this time. Case closed, no proof, I accept that.'

I wish I did, Keith thought; a spy, there was a thought.

It was the second week in October when Keith received the call. He and Barbara had just spent their customary autumn holiday in the Lakes which Keith found hugely frustrating. Barbara's idea of fun was to play bridge with the other residents, Keith's was to walk. Over the years they had compromised and now they largely went their own separate ways during the day, meeting only for dinner. It had been a time for rest and reflection and he had come back to Truro with renewed energy, ready to face whatever challenges lay ahead – but not this one, he had not expected this one. He had only been back at his desk half a day when his mobile phone rang. He looked at it and saw 'Miles I' on the screen and his heart flipped a beat.

'Miles?'

'Is that Chief Inspector Penrose?'

'Yes it is,' said Keith, 'how are you?'

'Not very good,' Miles said. He sounded very young and very hesitant.

'What's wrong?'

'Just about everything, the house is in uproar.'

'Why?' said Keith.

'I've just got back from college and there are two men here in the house, identical, both claiming to be my father. They've been shouting at each other all afternoon, my mother has taken to her bed and I just didn't know who else to ring. I don't know what to do, it's awful.'

'Two men, both claiming to be your father, I don't understand,' said Keith, who was starting to understand only too well.

'They look absolutely identical, it's creepy and both of them are claiming to be Sir Hugo.'

'And you really can't tell which is which?'

'I don't know, I can't bear it. I've come upstairs and left them to it,' Miles was beginning to cry. 'I'm so confused by it all. Could you come and sort it out, you're the sort of person who could I'm sure and I don't know who else to turn to.'

'I'm not sure if it can be me, Miles, but be strong and hang in there. I'll get something sorted out for you and I'll come back to you very shortly.'

'Sir, it's Keith Penrose.'

'Keith, how are you, how was your holiday?' said George Staple, leaning back in his chair.

'I've had a call from Miles Irving,' said Keith without preamble, 'he's in one hell of a state, sir. There appear to be two men at the family home both claiming to be Sir Hugo and both identical – to one another that is. What the hell is going on, sir? The boy is in a terrible state and I promised to help but obviously my hands are tied since you won't let me remain involved in the case.'

There was an edge of bitterness to Keith's voice which George Staple did not miss. 'Hang on a moment,' said the superintendent, 'let me get this straight. There are two men both claiming to be Sir Hugo, both looking alike and both at the family home currently?'

'That's right,' said Keith, 'It's obviously both twins I was trying to tell you about. We've got to do something to help that poor boy, he's fragile enough as it is.'

'I agree,' said George. 'Look, get on the motorway, Keith, right away and head up to London. I have to make a couple of phone calls and then I'll telephone you on the way and tell you exactly what's going on. Tell no one you're going, not even your wife, at least tell her you're going somewhere but not anything at all about the Irvings. Do I have your agreement to that?'

'Yes, of course, sir,' said Keith, 'and you want me to head up to London now?'

'This moment, I'll call you back.'

Keith grabbed his jacket and headed for the door, but not before ringing Miles, who answered immediately. 'I'm on my way,' he said.

It was a leap of faith – heaven knows what he would do if the super cancelled the trip – go anyway, he thought, defiantly.

18

It was a long journey up the A30 and the M5, a long journey to reflect on what on earth was going on and despite his mind twisting this way and that, Keith felt none the wiser when at last, on approaching the Sedgemoor Services, his phone flashed up a call from George Staple. He pulled off the motorway, towards the services and returned the call. The super's voice was very sombre but his message welcome.

'Keith, I'm really sorry to have kept you out of the loop for so long but I had my instructions and no choice but to follow them. We've never had any secrets between us before and I hope you will understand why I have to be less than frank with you this time.' Keith said nothing. 'Sir Hugo Irving was recruited by the KGB while he was in Cambridge but very soon turned double agent, cynically I imagine when he started to make money. Nonetheless, apparently, he has been extremely useful to our government over the years. Because of the size and commitment to his business, he has been very part-time but nonetheless he is highly valued by MI5.'

Keith couldn't believe what he was hearing. Felicity Paradise had got it right again. 'So how does all this fit in with the current situation, sir?'

George Staple took a deep breath. 'The disappearance on Porthmeor Beach was staged. At the time there was reason to suppose that the KGB might have rumbled Sir Hugo and he was in real danger. MI5 set up the surfing accident in a sufficiently professional way that you, and everyone else involved, were supposed to accept without question Sir Hugo's apparent drowning. Of course the added complication of the girl being murdered at the Irvings' home could not have been anticipated and was unfortunate.'

'So what happened to Hugo?' Keith asked. He was burning with resentment at the thought of wasting so much time trying to find a non-existent body.

'He was taken to a safe house, or at least he was until a few hours ago.'

'I'm getting more confused with this tale by the moment,' said Keith. 'I assume that during the last few weeks, it has been Bob Barnes from Tresco who has been masquerading as Sir Hugo. But why? He must have been a sitting duck for the KGB if they want Sir Hugo. Why on earth should his brother pretend to be him, it makes no sense?'

'Keith I'm not privy to the workings of MI5, like you I'm just a humble policeman, but as I understand it, they recruited Lady Irving to play along with Bob

Barnes in Sir Hugo's place. Lady Irving has been well aware of her husband's activities, had to have been, and whether it was MI5 who contacted Bob or Lady Irving suggesting a family get-together, I don't know. All I do know is Sir Hugo was getting restless at the safe house and more than a little fed up with his twin brother living the life of Riley and pretending to be him.'

'The last time I tried to make contact with the family,' said Keith, 'they were away.'

'Yes, I gather that MI5 sent Bob Barnes off to the wilds of Scotland so that he could have a teach-in on how to be Sir Hugo.'

'I still don't understand why he agreed to do it?' said Keith.

'Look Keith, time is short and we need to get this sorted out. It doesn't matter what Bob's motives are.' The super sounded rattled in a way Keith had never heard him before, 'I don't know the deal, Keith. Maybe Bob gets to lead a super-rich lifestyle which is a good enough offer to make him risk the KGB, thus keeping the real Sir Hugo safe – and it's Sir Hugo who has forty odd years of secrets which MI5 want kept that way.'

'So why am I being sent charging up the motorway to sort it all out?' Keith asked. 'I'm the person no one can trust, if you remember, why don't MI5 sort out their own bloody mess?'

'It's the boy, Miles, they're worried about. He seems to have a lot of faith in you, Keith, he wouldn't have called you otherwise. It's very important he doesn't blow Hugo's cover – and he might. There is no love lost between Miles and his father. Everyone seems to think you'll have a calming effect on the boy. Just go up there and see what's going on and report back. Do nothing.'

Mother and son were sitting in Miles's bedroom with the door locked trying to ignore the shouting match which had been going on two floors below.

'I thought identical twins were supposed to be especially close,' said Bettine smiling at her son to try and lighten the mood.

'Siblings aren't always close, so I understand – not that I'd know, I never had the opportunity to be with mine.' Miles was not returning the smile. His words sounded bitter; his large brown eyes, usually so warm and friendly, were cold and accusing.

'Oh Miles!' Bettine reached for his hand, but he snatched it away as if her touch would burn.

'You must have known I had a sister, you must have seen her, we shared a cot for God's sake. How did it feel taking me and leaving her alone – in that place? I've been to the orphanage, I've seen it for myself. I was told it is much better than it was … it was hell on earth. How could you do something so monstrous? How could you? How could you?' he hung his head, tears coursing down his face.

'We'd lost our own little girl. Adopting

Marianna would have felt like trying to replace her.'

'And what would have been wrong with that?' Miles spat out the words, his rage was almost tangible.

'Nursing Elizabeth through her short and painful life was the most terrible time. Your father was no help, he left me to cope alone with her suffering. It was agony, lying beside her as she fought for breath. I used to beg God or anyone who would listen to let me have her condition, to let me suffer. I couldn't bear to watch her pain and I couldn't bear to leave her alone with it, even for a second. When it was over, when she died, I was a wreck, my emotions seemed to have died with her, I was just an empty shell.'

She had Miles's attention now. She had never spoken to him of Elizabeth's death before, never opened up to him as she was doing now.

'Go on,' he said, the anger gone.

'Your father wanted a son, to carry on the business, and the name I suppose. We tried, but I had a miscarriage after miscarriage and each time I lost a baby, it felt …' she hesitated, 'like losing Elizabeth all over again. I was ill, I became very thin, in the end I couldn't even conceive … and then,' again she hesitated, looking up to meet Miles's gaze, seeking understanding, 'and then the Romanians shot their president on Christmas Day.'

There was along silence between them. The brothers' shouting could still be heard, but Miles and Bettine were oblivious to it now.

'It was love at first sight. I saw you and I was

238

healed. You gave me back my life, Miles. I loved you completely from the first moment the orphanage nurse put you in my arms.' It was Bettine's turn to cry now, great wracking sobs that shook her slender frame. Miles made no move to comfort her, but the hostility had quite gone.

'I loved you differently from Elizabeth, because you were different, but quite as much. People talk about nature and nurture, whether you can love a child you did not create as much as a birth child, believe me Miles, you can, you can. I would happily walk into the cannon's mouth for you, my darling. I would have done then, I would today. You are my boy.'

'But I was born someone else's boy and by the time I found out it was too late. What gave you the right to deny me the knowledge of who I am?' the anger was back.

'No right. I know that now, after what happened to poor Marianna. I realise I did you a terrible wrong by not telling you who you really were.'

'And your neglecting to tell me the truth cost Marianna her life.'

'Did it?' tears sprung into Bettine's eyes again.

'Of course it did. Do you think for one moment, I would have let things rest if I had known I had a sister left … left rotting in that place. If you had loved me as you say, you'd have realised we came as a package. What you did by separating us and not telling me the truth condemned Marianna to a life as

239

a prostitute and led without a shadow of doubt to her death.'

'Miles, I am so very, very, sorry to have caused you so much pain.' The simple words rang true.

'So why did you do it? Why not tell me I was adopted? Why the secrecy?

'Your father didn't want to make it public knowledge. You felt like mine; we just let things drift.'

'Knowing where my sister was?'

'I couldn't have adopted her, Miles. It really would have been like trying to replace Elizabeth; they were the same age, or would have been if Elizabeth had lived. I couldn't love a little girl who was not Elizabeth.'

'You could have tried. Anything would have been better than leaving her there. If there was no love from you, there would have been plenty from me to compensate and she would have been safe. Anyway you would have come to love her in time.'

'Maybe, but as she grew, I worried that I would resent her for being able to do all the things that Elizabeth never had the chance to do.'

'You wanted me to be a part of you, she was a part of me, therefore she was also a part of you. It makes no sense.'

'I know that now, Miles.'

'It's too late now.'

'Don't you think I know that too, but I still love you, still want to help and support you in any way I can. I didn't save your sister, but I did save you. The orphanage didn't want us to adopt you, they said you were too sick, that you would die soon.'

'And for that I am grateful. Is that what you want me to say?' Miles asked angrily.

'No, I want you to understand that I thought I was protecting you, that I did what I did out of love. I know you will never forgive me, but I want to believe that someday you might care for me again, just a little.'

Miles smiled and the woman sitting beside him basked in the warmth of the smile, daring to hope.

'I might be able to do that, Mum,' he said simply and took her hand.

They sat in silence on the bed, still holding hands, both lost in thought when there was an appalling crash and the raised voices reached a new crescendo.

'I hope they're not going to kill each other,' said Bettine, almost welcoming the disturbance below as it eased the tension between them.

'I don't mind if Bob kills Dad; that would be fine with me,' Miles said firmly

'Miles, that's a dreadful thing to say.'

'It's just that Bob being here has been so much …' he hesitated, groping for words.

'So much calmer, kinder and friendlier,' Bettine finished for him.

'He's a nice man, much nicer than Dad,' Miles agreed.

'It's odd isn't it? One twin has everything, the

other has nothing, but it is the twin with everything who seems so angry and resentful and the twin who has nothing in life seems to be calm and accepting.' There was a final shout and then silence.

'Oh, God,' said Bettine, 'what on earth has happened?'

They listened for a moment and then there was the slam of the front door.

'So one of them has left,' Miles said with a heavy sigh, 'I wonder which one?'

'If it's Bob who stayed, he'll be up to find us; if it's Dad, he'll be hitting the whisky bottle.'

After some persistent ringing the door was finally answered by Miles.

'Chief Inspector,' he said as if genuinely astounded to see him.

'Miles,' said Keith, 'are you alright?'

'Yes, yes fine.'

'You asked me to come and help you so I'm here,' said Keith.

Miles shook his head as if to clear his thoughts. 'Yes, of course, I'm sorry. I'm afraid I've brought you on quite a wild goose chase, everything is fine now.' He made as if to close the door.

'Hang on one minute, young man. I've just driven three hundred and fifty miles at your request. Now I'm here, I need to come in and satisfy myself that all is well.'

Without waiting for a reaction Keith mounted the steps and pushed past Miles into the house. 'Where is everyone,' he demanded.

'In the drawing room,' Miles said, clearly apprehensive.

'It's alright,' said Keith, 'I know my way.'

Sir Hugo and Lady Irving were sitting on either side of the fire place, apparently in earnest conversation which broke off immediately Keith entered the room.

'What the …?' Sir Hugo began, rising to his feet. Lady Irving rose too and stood uncertainly, glancing anxiously at both men.

'Sorry to disturb you, Sir Hugo, but young Miles sent for me. I gather there has been some trouble between you and your twin brother.'

'I'm not Hugo Irving,' said "Hugo", confusingly. My name is Bob Barnes, I'm Hugo's brother, and you are?' Rather theatrically, he extended his hand formally in a greeting.

Keith shook hands; the likeness to Hugo was total. 'Chief Inspector Keith Penrose, sir, of Devon and Cornwall Constabulary. I was involved in your, I mean your brother's disappearance. Where is your brother?'

'I don't know,' Bob Barnes answered, testily. 'He came here in a foul temper, after all I'm doing for him, accusing me of everything under the sun, and then left.' He glanced at his watch. 'He left about three hours ago, around midday.'

'To go where?' Keith asked

'I don't know, don't care after the way he behaved.'

'And you, Lady Irving, do you know where he's gone?' Bettine shook her head. 'You are both aware that he is in grave danger?' Keith was losing patience.

'He's not in grave danger,' Bob said, 'it's me who is running the risk of being grabbed or worse by the KGB. I assume you are aware that my brother is a spy?' Keith nodded. 'Then you'll know that Hugo has a safe house to go to and that I am the one in the firing line, I'm his decoy.'

'Why did you agree to do it?' Keith asked, curiously.

'Unlike my brother, I am not a spy, Chief Inspector, so forgive me for becoming confused by what seems an increasingly complex situation. As I understand it, the KGB got wind of the fact that my brother's disappearance was staged, and that he is alive, well and extremely aggressive – at least he is towards me. MI5 are apparently in top level talks with the KGB trying to negotiate some sort of spy amnesty. MI5 are holding a Russian who the KGB want back very badly – so badly that they are prepared to leave my brother alone if they get their man.'

'So how is this particular charade supposed to end?' Keith asked.

'If I survive and the negotiations are successful,

then at some stage in the future, Hugo will seamlessly take up the reins of his old life and I will disappear.'

'Back to Tresco?' Keith asked.

'No, no, I won't have to work again, that's part of the deal. A nice little cottage somewhere – Dartmoor, probably, and a modest but adequate pension from a grateful government.'

'The arrangement seems rather hard on the family,' Keith said, gesturing towards Bettine and Miles who were now standing very close together and seemed anxious to distance themselves from Bob's explanation.

'Bob's been very good to us,' Miles burst out suddenly. 'He's been really understanding about my adoption, about Marianna and he's been extremely kind and helpful to my mother.' A look passed between Miles and Bob – one of sheer loathing. It was in such complete contrast to the words Miles had spoken, Keith whirled round to Bettine.

'Are you sure that this man is Bob Barnes and not your husband, Hugo Irving?'

'Absolutely sure,' she replied in a small voice.

'It's all a complete cock up!' Miles exploded again. He indicated towards Bob with a nod of the head. 'He knows. It wasn't MI5 who recruited Bob, it was the KGB pretending to be MI5. They wanted to flush out Hugo's whereabouts and guessed by bringing him "back from the dead", he would break cover. They judged rightly as it turned out – Hugo couldn't bear to just stand back and watch his brother taking his place – enjoying the fruits of his labours, would be how he saw it.'

'Enough, Miles, you have no idea what you're talking about.' Bob took a step forward as if he was going to strike the boy.

Keith moved quickly between them. 'Is this right, did the KGB recruit you?' he asked.

'Of course not, the boy is talking nonsense, as usual.'

'I'm not, I'm right, Chief Inspector, and now he's out there somewhere and is going to be killed unless we do something quickly.'

'Who's out there?' Keith demanded.

'There was complete silence, no one answered, even Bob seemed lost for words. Clearly something was wrong, terribly wrong, but before Keith could marshal his thoughts, his mobile rang. It was Superintendent George Staple.

'Keith, where are you?'

'With the Irvings, sir.'

'Can you put yourself somewhere private for a moment?'

'Yes,' said Keith. He looked at the three of them, standing in silent tableau, looking strangely trapped. 'It's my superintendent,' he said, 'can I take this call somewhere else?'

'Of course,' said Miles, 'I'll show you through to the dining room.'

With the door shut firmly behind him, Keith crossed the room and stood by the window looking out on to the street. 'Yes, sir.'

'I've had a call from the Met, they've just pulled the body of Sir Hugo Irving out of the Serpentine.'

'His dead body, sir?'

'Quite dead. It appears he drowned, the general feeling is it was probably an accident or suicide.'

'Sir, are you sure it is Sir Hugo because I have grave doubts that it is?' Keith's voice was urgent and tense. 'Who identified the body, how does anyone know which brother it is?'

'MI5 have taken charge and they have confirmed that it is Sir Hugo. The brother, Bob, is still in the house with you, I understand.'

'Yes, only I don't think it is Bob and I'm sure it isn't an accident. I think …'

'Keith, enough. I'd like you to break the news to the family that Sir Hugo is dead and when you are satisfied that everyone is calm, particularly Miles who I understand is something of a loose cannon, I would like you to leave and come straight back to Cornwall. This is an order, Keith, from the very highest level. Break the news and then so far as you are concerned, the case is closed. Have I made myself absolutely clear?'

'As crystal, sir.' Keith said, heavily.

For some minutes, Keith stood by the window staring out with sightless eyes ahead of him. Over the years he had told many people of the death of a loved one. Even as a young copper he had been singled out for the job because of his compassion and ability to communicate with people. In his mind's eye he saw a long procession of happy faces crumbling into shock, misery and disbelief as he stumblingly told them what had just happened to their husband, wife, mother, father, son, daughter, sister, brother, friend. Normally they became apprehensive the moment they saw a policeman standing on their doorstep but he remembered one particular occasion when a young woman had answered the door and assumed he was the policeman who had agreed to come and talk at her children's school the following day. Before he could explain anything, she had ushered him into the kitchen. A baby sat in a highchair playing with bricks, a couple of older children were doing homework round the kitchen table and the woman was clearly in the middle of baking. It was the perfect domestic scene and he had come to tell her that her husband had just died in a motorway pile up.

He took a deep breath and squared his shoulders. He was a policeman with a job to do; he'd been given his instructions, it was his job to carry them out, whatever his own personal views. With a heavy heart he opened the dining room door and headed back across the hallway.

His expression must have given him away. 'What is it?' Bettine jumped out of her chair.

'Lady Irving, I've just had some very bad news. It appears your husband has drowned.'

'What are you talking about?' Miles strode across the room. 'Is this some sick joke, we've done the drowning bit once already.'

'No Miles, it's not a sick joke, his body has just been pulled out of the Serpentine. No one knows exactly the cause of death at the moment but it would appear that he may have decided to take his own life.'

'Are you absolutely sure about this?' Lady Irving asked tremulously.

'Yes.'

She crumpled onto the chair and began to weep. Bob made no move to comfort her, indeed he said nothing at all.

'MI5 have taken charge of the body,' Keith said, 'I imagine the Met will need you to identify him in the fullness of time, sir.'

Bob nodded curtly and then met Keith's eye. 'I think in the circumstances it would be best if you left us now with our grief.'

'Yes, of course,' said Keith. He turned to Miles. Miles was white as a sheet, tears were streaming down his face. He was staring in anguish at his mother. Keith longed to go to the boy, to give him a hug, to talk to him, to reassure him, he was also hoping for an outburst, a denial, some indication that they had got the wrong man. Miles avoided eye contact, he hung his head, he clearly had nothing to say.

'I'll see myself out then.' No one seemed to hear him, he turned and walked across the hall towards the front door.

His hand was on the doorknob when he heard Miles' voice. 'Chief Inspector,' he turned and Miles came towards him. 'Thanks,' he said, 'thanks for coming.'

Keith dropped his voice. 'Miles, is there anything you want to tell me about all of this?'

Miles glanced over his shoulder. Already the figure of Bob Barnes was in the doorway staring across the hall towards them.

'No,' Miles said, 'no nothing at all.'

The funeral of Sir Hugo Irving was a grand affair. There was much talk of his contribution to British Industry, his charity work and how in the last few months of his life, he had been reconciled with his twin brother from whom he was separated at birth. The papers were full of pictures of Lady Irving, Miles and Uncle Bob and then, as is the way of such things, within twenty-four hours of the funeral the Irvings were yesterday's news. There had been no hint of Sir Hugo's life as a spy. The verdict on his death was deemed to be accidental, the general feeling being that he had never fully recovered from his amnesia. Case closed, finished – Keith had one final attempt to try to discuss the matter with his superintendent and was told in no uncertain terms that speculation was fruitless.

PROLOGUE

Felicity was in a state. Mel's wedding was less than a month away and she had nothing to wear and far more important, neither had the bride. Felicity's pregnancies had always been miserable affairs – there has been sickness for the first three months and then she had felt exhausted and achy for the remaining six. Mel's pregnancy, by contrast, appeared to be glorious. Having survived early morning sickness, she had gone into a sort of relaxed and laid back mode, serene and calm, which was completely out of character with the normal Mel and was most disconcerting for everyone who knew her. The shopping trip really couldn't be put off much longer but Felicity hated shopping for clothes, as did Mel, and so was very relieved when the phone rang.

'I wondered what you were up to today?' said Keith.

'Trying to persuade myself I need to go shopping

for clothes,' said Felicity, 'for the wedding. I just can't get myself worked up to do it – not the wedding I mean – the buying of clothes, I hate it.'

'How about lunch instead then,' said Keith, 'I've got some good news for you.'

'I'd like that,' said Felicity, 'which means I won't have time to go into Truro for clothes shopping, so you've totally solved my problem for today.'

'Excellent,' said Keith, 'shall I come to St Ives?'

'I've so fallen in love with the Mount, I think if I'm not going shopping, I might go over to Marazion to do some sketching. We could meet there, which would be easier parking for you, too.'

'Perfect. Twelve-thirty, Godolphin Arms?'

'I'll be there,' said Felicity.

It was too cold for the terrace but they managed to get a table in the restaurant by the window.

'The last time I had a meal here,' said Felicity, a little wistfully, 'was the night Orlando died.'

'I'm sorry,' said Keith, 'maybe we should have chosen a different location.'

'No, it's fine, I'm just being stupid. Tell me, what is your good news?'

'It's about Anya,' said Keith. 'Obviously, she's had to stay in this country to testify against Jackson, when the case goes to trial next week. There's a nice family who live on the outskirts of Bodmin. They've done quite a lot of fostering over the years and currently have one foster child and three of their own, the wife is the elder sister of a friend of Carly's. Anyway, Anya has been staying with them and helping out with the children and has proved to be really good. They also have a smallholding – she loves the farm work too and is a real worker. They would like her to stay permanently as a member of their family, and so would she. There are all sorts of different adoption and fostering contracts these days and apparently Social Services are all for it so it looks like little Anya might end up with a family of her own after all.'

'That's marvellous news,' said Felicity, 'thank you so much for telling me. Do you think it would be possible for me to visit her? I would so much like to keep in touch.'

'I'm sure it would and equally sure she'd love to see you. She's not safe yet, but she is doing a great service to this country by helping nail a rat like Jackson. The trial is going to be very traumatic for her and we can't possibly allow her to give evidence and then be shipped back to Romania to goodness knows what sort of future. The family are perfectly prepared to be responsible for her financially, they are aware of her background and they are used to dealing with traumatised children – let's face it, despite the life she has been forced to lead Anya is little more than a child herself – it's an ideal situation.'

'How is she getting on with the language?' Felicity asked.

'Brilliantly, apparently, she's a natural linguist like most Romanians I believe. She's very bright.'

'One happy ending at any rate. I hope Miles will be alright, I think about him often,' said Felicity.

'Me too,' said Keith.

'I think you became quite fond of him when you were in Romania, didn't you?'

'Yes,' said Keith, 'he's a nice boy with an awful lot on his plate.'

'I still think there's something about the whole case which stinks,' said Felicity. 'The ending was too neat, I'm sorry, I know I shouldn't go on and on, you must be heartily sick of my theories but what I think happened ...'

'Please, please, God, spare me from another Paradise theory!' Keith put his hands together in silent prayer.

'Not a chance,' said Felicity cheerfully. 'I think Sir Hugo was a spy and that the body found in the Serpentine wasn't Sir Hugo at all, it was poor old Bob. I think Sir Hugo is now pretending to be Bob and all the powers that be are involved in a cover up.'

Keith stared at her; she had all his attention now, the teasing of a moment ago was quite gone. 'Is that all?' he asked.

'Isn't it enough? I know I am probably way out of line but everything about Sir Hugo fits my theory – Cambridge, communist turned capitalist, going missing like that and then reappearing – I bet the whole thing was set up – it was, wasn't it, I can see it in your face, I'm right, aren't I?'

'Stop, stop!' Keith let out a sigh and smiled at her a little sadly. 'I can see there will be no peace until I tell you what I know. I suppose I can justify discussing the case with you because without you, we would never have known about the brother. I suppose MI5 did, but we lowly policemen would have had no idea of his existence but for you.'

'MI5, I knew it! So he was a spy?'

Keith nodded. 'And his disappearance was staged. He was a double agent apparently and MI5 believed the KGB had rumbled him and so removed him to a safe house.'

'Goodness,' said Felicity, 'you really could have been an actor if you hadn't joined the police force.'

'What on earth makes you say that?"I really believed you were looking for Sir Hugo when he disappeared, you were very convincing.'

'I was very convincing,' said Keith, crossly, 'because I really was looking for Sir Hugo and wasting my time and the taxpayer's money. My super did not consider it necessary to take me into his confidence.'

'So when did you find out what was really going on?' Felicity asked, aware that she had inadvertently touched a very raw nerve.

'I still haven't, not really. Bob, if it was Bob at the house the day Sir Hugo died, told me he had been recruited by MI5 to take Sir Hugo's place while they did some sort of deal with the KGB. However, Miles seemed to think that Bob had been tricked and in fact had been recruited by the KGB, posing as MI5.'

'Why?'

'You may well ask. According to Miles, the KGB were hoping to encourage Sir Hugo to reappear, infuriated by his brother taking over his life, presumably so they could grab him or murder him, who knows.'

'I certainly can see that Sir Hugo would not take kindly to festering away in a safe house, while his brother was having a high old time living his life,' Felicity agreed.

'That was Miles's theory too. To be honest, I don't think it matters one way or the other who recruited who to do what. There is no such thing as a gentleman spy these days. They're all a lot of gangsters, vicious, nasty people who get more kicks out of torture and murder than they do from serving Queen and country.'

'That's a bit harsh, isn't it?' Felicity protested. 'I don't think Hugo was a murderer and a torturer.'

'No you're right but I think he may have sacrificed his brother to save his own skin.'

'So you do think it was Bob they hauled out of the Serpentine?'

'Yes I do, but I have been told at the highest level to drop the case, so there really is nothing more I can do. I believe Bob was killed but by who, I have no idea. It could have been the KGB, probably the most likely candidate, but it could have been MI5 or even Hugo – he had time to do it before I turned up at the house.'

'That's terrible, but I thought it was an accident. Are you sure which ever brother it was, really was murdered.'

'Yes, of course, it was a complete cover up, not even the Met were given the opportunity to view the body.'

'Wouldn't it be possible to DNA the surviving twin to prove who he is?'

Keith shook his head. 'It would be possible to DNA the surviving twin but it would prove nothing. Identical twins have the same DNA.'

'Do they?' said Felicity, 'I didn't realise that. What about fingerprints?'

'Ah,' said Keith, 'fingerprints are similar but not the same; no two people in the world have the same fingerprints.'

'So it would be possible …' Felicity began, but then she frowned, '… but you'd have to have something to compare them with.'

'I did a little checking,' said Keith, 'back in his days in Bradford, Bob Barnes was done for drink driving, as a result of which he never drove again, but he was fingerprinted at the time.'

'So you believe Sir Hugo is pretending to be Bob to save himself from the KGB, but if so surely Lady Irving and Miles must be in on the plot.'

'Yes, of course,' Keith agreed, 'but why, I'm not sure. They were both badly frightened when I saw them. I suppose they could have been got at by either the KGB or MI5, threatened with heaven knows what if they didn't keep their mouths shut. The man at the house that night was certainly more like Hugo than I imagine Bob to be and clearly Miles loathed him. Funny that, it is possible I have never actually met Bob Barnes.'

Felicity sat back in her chair triumphant. 'So are you going to admit that my theory was right all along?'

'I couldn't possibly comment,' said Keith. 'However for Miles's sake, I would very much welcome the opportunity to fingerprint the current incumbent of the Irvings' Notting Hill house.'

'Maybe you'll get the chance one day,' said Felicity.

'Maybe I will,' agreed Chief Inspector Penrose.